......it all Started as a Joke

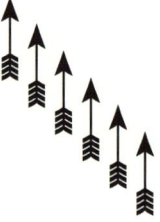

4

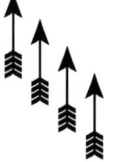

©RAY MOND 2022
The Blind Archer. Copyright 2022 by Ray Mond. All rights reserved. No part of this book may be used or reproduced in any manner whatsoever without the written permission except in the case of brief quotations embodied in critical articles and reviews. Any resemblance to anyone living or dead is purely coincidental. But, if you really have a fucking dog that talks to you and tells you where to hit the bullseye in your Archery competition... wow.. first..that's utterly amazing. Second. Gawd dam you can't be original these fucking days. Fuck me. Ugh.
Library of Congress Cataloging-in-Publication Data has been applied for The Blind Archer.

And since I have your attention in this little public statement. For fuck sakes..... We need term limits in fucking congress for fuck sakes... Sorry but, reading about congress men and woman who have been in the white house for 60 years + in congress doesn't tell me that you are experience and are looking at my best interest. HAHAHA BULLSHIT!...It just tells me that you love power and you don't want to let go. This message is especially to the congress men and woman who have been in congress for so many decades that I lost count. Do the AMERICAN people a favor and fucking RETIRE! We need TERM LIMITS in Congress

   Copyrighted 2022 and WGAw# 2142240

   ISBN

   Cover Design: Ray Mond

@ZIPPER4000

www.zipper4000.com

Dedication *11*

Prologue *13*

Chapter 1: POPPING OUT *14*

Chapter 2: THE ONE OF THE ONE OF THE ONE. *20*

Chapter 3: GRANT DAVIS. *24*

Chapter 4: I SEE NO FUTURE *32*

Chapter 5: CANTGETRITE *36*

Chapter 6: STAY THE COURSE *44*

Chapter 7: DESTINY HISTORY SAVIOR *50*

Chapter 8: LAPORSHA *56*

Chapter 9: DRIVING WHILE BLIND *68*

Chapter 10: RUBEE *74*

Chapter 11: CINDY YUMI *80*

Chapter 12: JIGGLY JIGGLY *84*

Chapter 13: FAKIN' MOMMY *92*

Chapter 14: TRAINING REVEAL *98*

Chapter 15: WHISKEY SHOT *104*

Chapter 16: MICKEY D's, 100K, and COCAINE! *110*

Chapter 17: TUNE IN TOKYO! COME IN TOKYO! *120*

Chapter 18: "DANCIN' IN COCAINE" *128*

Chapter 19: LET THAT BITCH FLY! *134*

Chapter 20: SHE'S ALREADY DEAD, DON'T PANIC? *142*

Chapter 21: COFFEE GINGER PIZZA? *146*

Chapter 22: VEGAS IS CALLING! *154*

Chapter 23: OH CANADA *166*

Chapter 24: THE CRYPTO GANG *174*

Chapter 25 00 ABOB *182*

Chapter 26: BINGBONG BOOMER *188*

Chapter 27: MACK CHAZY *192*

Chapter 28: YUG DAB BATTLE *196*

Chapter 29: AMERICAN EAGLE STAR *208*

Chapter 30: BROKEN BOW *214*

Chapter 31: SWEDISH SENSATION *218*

Chapter 32: THE BLIND ARCHER *224*

Chapter 33: BULLSEYE'S BACK! *232*

Chapter 34: I SEE YOU *236*

How The Blind Archer came to be: *240*

About The Author: Ray Mond *251*

10

DEDICATION

I dedicate this book to Kenny Hoang. Best Yorke Ever!

Of course, I dedicate this book to my parents; what kind of an asshole puts their dog dedication above their parents is beyond me.

I also want to dedicate to Ryan, who was there at the beginning, when this was just a joke of an idea that had me laughing for six days straight.

Judy, thank you for buying my first book... as you can tell, I edited the book lol. I'm sending you the new 1st, then 2nd and 3rd later this month. (It's Jan 3rd 2022 - 2:01 AM Eastern time)

To my writing friend, Jeff Bonilla. A real world-acclaimed author for, "Terminal Hitman."

Randy Ruiz, Alvin, Kinich, Mark, Denise, Milad, SteveD.V., Nancy, Roland, Patricia, Ada, Kevin and Q

12

PROLOGUE

"I FINALLY FEEL LIKE I'M STARTING TO SEE AGAIN"
PISSING INTO THE WIND -UNKNOWN BLIND MAN

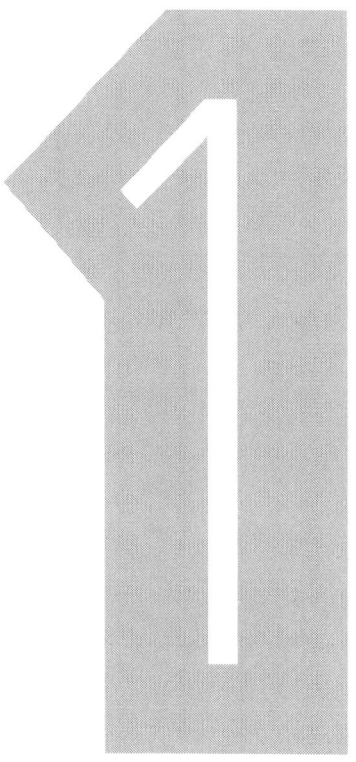

FADE IN:

EXT. VERMONT STATE FAIR - DAY

The 66th Annual World Archery competition in Rutland, Vermont at the state fairground with hundreds of spectators in the stands cheering as Mack Chazy, a very hairy Jamaican with dreads to his waist, grabs the mic.

                    MACK CHAZY
          Welcome back, and if you're just joining us, I'd
          like to welcome you to the 66th annual world
          archery competition in the great state of Vermont
          sponsored by DogeCoin. We are witnessing
          history in the making folks with the great Don
          "Bullseye" Davis, who has never missed a
          bullseye and looks like he will become the 7th
          time world championship Archery, master.

DON "BULLSEYE" DAVIS, 45 chubby hillbilly looking gent, graying goatee and buck-teeth, taps his Bluetooth while pulling out an arrow from his quiver.

                    DON "BULLSEYE" DAVIS
          Mama... double the wager with those Vegas
          people you talk to on the computer.

Don takes a deep breath.

                    DON "BULLSEYE" DAVIS
          That's right, and I won't miss.

Don aligns the arrow.

                    DON "BULLSEYE" DAVIS
          Loan it to me, Mama. I'm guaranteed to win.

Don pulls back the arrow.

                    DON "BULLSEYE" DAVIS
          But, Mama... we can triple our monies, and we
          are set for life. Me, you, Grant and Bingbong. I'm
          good for it.

Releases the arrow.

17

                    DON "BULLSEYE" DAVIS
I'm a sure thing. 7th time Champion, here I come.

Arrow hits bullseye.

                    DON "BULLSEYE" DAVIS
Stop with the sixes superstition, Mama! We can finally triple our monies with this hear Doge Coin winnings because I'm Bullseye!

                    MACK CHAZY
Bullseye!... Bullseye!... The Don has done it again. Amazing folk. Just utterly amazing! I'm MACK CHAZY reporting from the Vermont state fair.

INGRID, a 25-year-old Swedish blondie with huge 36DDD breast walking towards Don, quickly pulls out an arrow and hits a bullseye.

                    MACK CHAZY
Ingrid, the Swedish sensation, answers the call but, it doesn't matter, folks! Don is the 7th time returning champion, and all he has to do is hit any target per rules regulation.

Dan takes out an arrow and pulls back.

                    INGRID
Bullseye!

Dan turns around.

Ingrid lifts her top, exposing her huge 36DDD breast.

Dan's eyes widen while his mouth waters.

Dan's fingers slip, releasing the ARROW.

An AMERICAN EAGLE

BREAKING THE 4TH WALL

Flies directly to the camera.

The Arrow, frozen in middle-air, was heading towards the spectators.

All Spectators are frozen, screaming.

      AMERICAN EAGLE
I know what you're thinking. I should stream a different Netflix movie. Well, that makes you a quitter and have a negative outlook on life. So If you're always thinking you're having a bad day, remember someone in this world has it much worse, so pipe down, shut the fuck up!...and enjoy this stupid comedy.

An Emergency broadcast system banner appears at the bottom. "This movie isn't going to win any Oscars."

      END OF 4TH WALL

The Arrow flies past the American Eagle, almost hitting the Eagle.

Spectators scream.

A GUST OF WIND forces the Arrow to switch directions and heads straight towards GRANT DAVIS' face, 24, who's sitting next to his 9-month pregnant wife, SUZY GRANT, 22

The Arrow Penetrate Grant's face, plucking his eyes out of their sockets.

The Arrow ricochets off of Grant's face hitting the American Eagle in mid-air.

American Eagle falls to the ground with the Arrow empaled in its body while having Grants' eyeballs attached.

Eagle dies.

Spectators scream in horror.

MACK CHAZY'S MIC DROPS

2

THE ONE OF THE ONE OF THE ONE

INT. UNDERGROUND FIGHT ARENA - NIGHT

Super: 5 YEARS LATER - PRESENT DAY - MONGOLIA CHINA

Dan "BULLSEYE" Davis wearing a woman's dress and sporting real 36DD Breast, faces off against 6 FIGHTERS.

KEMOSABE 81, dressed in an all white hoodie robe, jumps into the ring.

                    DON "BULLSEYE" DAVIS
    Master Kemosabe!

Kemosabe doges Fighter #1's punches.

                    KEMOSABE
    You disappoint me Bullseye.

Don grabs the Fighter #1's fist while his left 36DD breast uppercuts Fighter #1 out of the ring.

Fighter #1 flies over the crowd.

Crowd goes wild.

>   DON "BULLSEYE" DAVIS
>   (off of Kemosabe's remark)
>   I was supposed to be the one.

Kemosabe doges Fighter #2's kick.

>   KEMOSABE
>   You are the one!

Kemosabe doges another kick.

>   KEMOSABE
>   You're just not the one of the one of the one.

Fighter #2 lands a kick across Don's face.

Don grabs Fighter #2's leg and does a Flying Calif Kick.

>   DON "BULLSEYE" DAVIS
>   What does that make you?

>   KEMOSABE
>   (ducks)
>   The one.

Fighter #3, missing Kemosabe, tackles Dan to the ground.

Dan stumbles up and does a clothesline move, pounding Fighter #3 to the ground.

>   DON "BULLSEYE" DAVIS
>   Then who am I?

                    KEMOSABE
    The one of the one.

Kemosabe doges Fighter #3's punch.

                    DON "BULLSEYE" DAVIS
    Who's the one of the one of the one.

Don doges all punches

                    KEMOSABE
                (doges a punch)
    Your son. Grant

Don head punts Fighter #3 to the ground.

EXT. BASEBALL FIELD - NIGHT

Super: 6 YEARS PRIOR - NEW YORK

GRANT DAVIS 23, on the mound pitching for the Minor League Baseball team, BUFFALO BISONS.

VICK THOMPSON, a baseball player for Calgary Cannons, prepares to steal Third

Grant looks back at Vick and prepares to pitch.

BASEBALL ANNOUNCER
                    (O.S.)
          Bottom of the 6th, one out, and Vicks Thompson
          on second after successfully stealing, and here's
          the wind-up.

The batter hits the ball straight at Grant's face.

Grant catches the ball with his bare hand and immediately flings the ball towards second, tagging out Vick Thompson.

                    BASEBALL ANNOUNCER
                    (O.S.)
          Double play by Grant Davis catching that rocket.
          No gloves are required as he throws it to second,
          tagging out Vick the stealer Thompson. This kid is
          impressive. Look out, MLB.

SUZY DAVIS, 21, joins the cheers in the stand.

INT. GRANT'S CAR - NIGHT

Suzy rubs her belly

                    SUZY
          A girl, I'm thinking Bella. Boomer if it's a boy.

                    GRANT
          Coach told me that the Yankee's scout was in the
          bleachers tonight.

                    SUZY
          Even though you lost tonight, I know you got their
          attention tonight.

Suzy pulls down grant's hat.

SUZY (CONTINUOUS)
Mr. All-Star Pitcher for the New York Yankees!

Grant kisses Suzy's wedding ring and stares into Suzy's eyes.

SUZY
(staring back)
You have beautiful eyes.

INT. GRANT'S TRAILER - NIGHT

SUPER: 9 MONTHS LATER

Small trailer in a trailer park community where

Don, Rubee, Grant, and Suzy Grant are celebrating Grant's birthday at the dinner table.

Suzy covering Grant's eyes.

SUZY
No peeking.

Suzy uncovers Grant's eyes, who is about to blow out a cookie birthday cake.

RUBEE
Make a wish.

SUZY
(whispering to herself)
Wish to no longer live in a trailer.

Grant blows out all the candles while staring at Suzy.

RUBEE
          I'm proud of you. You have a vision of what you
          want to be and you are going after it.

Suzy and Grant tease each other with ice cream.

                    SUZY
          I just hope we aren't stuck in this trailer for long.

                    GRANT
          Ok, I heard it...You know I have to be close to the
          team.

                    SUZY
          Another year?

Don notions at Rubee.

                    DON "BULLSEYE" DAVIS
          Let us give the birthday boy and future mother a
          little private time.

EXT. GRANT'S TRAILER - NIGHT

                    RUBEE
          I can't take your bet this time.

                    DON "BULLSEYE" DAVIS
          You're my bookie.

                    RUBEE
          I'm also your mother and you've been winning
          none stop, Vegas doesn't like losing.

DON "BULLSEYE" DAVIS
Not my fault that I can't miss.

RUBEE
I'm serious, son. Vegas odds don't like losing.

DON "BULLSEYE" DAVIS
I grab the arrow, align the arrow, I let go of the arrow. The arrow hits the bullseye. Not once do you think, Oh, he missed because of Vegas. This isn't the NBA, mom! And how is Vegas going to manipulate the game of archery?

RUBEE
Lets cool down. It just doesn't feel right. You're just too hot right now.

DON "BULLSEYE" DAVIS
The prize money will be given in DogeCoin and it is at .66 cents, and it's expected to rise to one dollar by the end of this week. I can make an extra .44 cents on the dollar if we bet on me.

RUBEE
Now you're talking about speculation gambling to gambling odds. You don't have the money to cover the bets either.

DON "BULLSEYE" DAVIS
I can finally get Grant a home and help you with your surgery. I haven't missed. It's a sure thing.

RUBEE
I'm not dying plus you're not a crypto expert either Mr. I don't miss a target.

DON "BULLSEYE" DAVIS
We will be if you don't take the bet.

RUBEE
Tomorrow is June 6, and it's Grant's birthday, plus you're 6x champion. I don't like it. I have a terrible feeling. You don't want to owe money to the Crypto gang.

Grant walks out of his trailer.

GRANT
What are you two bickering about?

DON "BULLSEYE" DAVIS
Are you coming to my tournament tomorrow?

GRANT
Why? You can win with your eyes close. It's not even entertaining.

DON "BULLSEYE" DAVIS
I can take you out for your birthday dinner.

GRANT
Sure, but I can't stay long. I have a game that night.

RUBEE
Two athletes in the family.

DON "BULLSEYE" DAVIS
If you keep pitching the way you are. I'll be the one begging to see you play at the nationals.

GRANT
I have been playing in the minors for three years now and getting frustrated.

RUBEE
Don't lose sight. You have a vision of what you want, and once you lose your vision. It's game over. Any MLB team will be lucky to have you. It takes time.

                    GRANT
Thanks, grandma.

                    DON "BULLSEYE" DAVIS
              (towards Rubee)
So is that a yes?

                    RUBEE
No.

                    GRANT
It's getting late, and I can barely keep my eyes open. I'm calling it a night.

I SEE NO FUTURE

INT. GRANT'S TRAILER - MORNING

Super: PRESENT DAY - VERMONT

KITCHEN

Can't you see by The Notorious B.I.G. is being played as

BINGBONG 6-Year old Vietnamese boy opens up the refrigerator, pushes aside

A FROZEN PICKLE JAR FILLED WITH GRANT'S EYES. WE CAN SEE THE OPTIC NERVES ARE STILL CONNECTED TO THE RETINA.

Bingbong moves a wad of cash behind the pickle jar and pulls out frozen food.

Bingbong is dancing while cooking.

GRANT'S BEDROOM

The loud noises from the kitchen wakes up GRANT DAVIS 29 wearing a cloth covering his eyes.

KITCHEN

Bingbong has completed multiple food orders while distributing them to the many UBER EATS DELIVERY PEOPLE that walk into the trailer.

                        GRANT
               (towards the wall)
        Morning son.

                    BINGBONG
        Turn around, Grant.

Grant turns around but walks into the kitchen's island.

                    BINGBONG
        I made you a lunch to go, Wagyu Beef Tartare with a side of Bing Fries.

Bingbong doesn't wait for Grant's acknowledgment as he places the lunch container on the table and continues to cook, dance while updating his website and posting pictures to his TWITTER and INSTAGRAM account.

Grant grabs his lunch and walks into the wall.

5

CANTGETRITE
chapter JUST
CANTGETRITE

INT. AMC THEATERS - AFTERNOON

Grant wearing a blue headband covering his empty eye ballsocket, sporting an AMC t-shirt with the name tag: GRANT, and is working as a ticket taker.

A COUPLE OF KIDS quietly walk past Grant, giggling as they run into a theatre number 7

CANTGETRITE, 5'5" black man wearing SUNGLASSES walks out of theatre number 1991 with a huge bucket of popcorn, candy, ice cream, and drinks.

                    GRANT
          Aren't you afraid?

CantGetRite licking his fingers while ripping movie tickets and grabbing a handful of popcorn, and munching on it.

CANTGETRITE
Nope

GRANT
Germs?

CANTGETRITE
I welcome them.

GRANT
I'm wondering what the manager wants with both the of us.

CANTGETRITE
My ass is grass you'll remain here.

GRANT
You just started 6 hours ago.

CantGetRite's hotdog falls on the ground.

CANTGETRITE
10-second rule.

CantGetRite blows dust off the hotdog and takes a passionate bite off the already bitten hotdog.

GRANT
You don't sound so upset. Why?

CantGetRite continues to finish his hotdog while taking new customer's tickets.

CANTGETRITE
You should get you one of those seeing eye dogs.

GRANT
I have an appointment today and it's been such a long time waiting.

CANTGETRITE
Would you still be responsible for picking up his shit?

GRANT
I don't know how I can when I can't see.

CANTGETRITE
I feel like this dog might give you more problems than you can chew but, if you can swing it. Get a bitch to grab a bitch so you ain't a bitch you know. Bitches bring bitches. The first one is always the hardest.

Grant is slightly annoyed knowing that he has avoided the main question.

An AMC SUPERVISOR motions Grant and CantGetRite to follow him.

Cantgetrite notices an unattended pretzel on the counter and grabs it as he follows the supervisor.

GRANT
How can you eat at a time now?

CANTGETRITE
It's going to be my last time ever enjoying movie snacks without having to take out a loan. Gotta enjoy my last moments in this place.

GRANT

No it won't.

CANTGETRITE

Gentlemen's bet?

GRANT

You're on.

AMC MANAGER'S OFFICE - CONTINUOUS

Typical movie theater office with movie posters and a long wood table.

AMC MANAGER
(playfully stern)

Grant.

GRANT
(sarcastically playful)

Lindsay.

CantGetRite immediately notices the tension in the air and starts to finish his popcorn slowly while watching the conversation.

AMC MANAGER

The company is merging ticket taking with guest services and, unfortunately, going to have to let you go.

GRANT

I understand.

AMC MANAGER
We wish you the best.

GRANT
I know you do.

AMC MANAGER
I do

GRANT
Ok

CantgetRite hasn't stopped eating popcorn.

AMC Manager looks at CantgetRite.

AMC MANAGER
You must be the new hire, heard so much good things about you that I like to offer you a supervisor position.

CantgetRite is frozen in shock with his hand still in the popcorn tub.

Grant picks up his envelope.

Grant and AMC MANAGER exchange look.

Grant pulls out a dollar bill from his pocket and hands it to CantgetRite.

CantgetRite grabs it with a new sense of accomplishment.

AMC Manger walks towards Cantgetrite.

AMC MANAGER
Well, now that we have some privacy.

Cantgetrite is now slightly confused about what's going on and immediately figures it out.

AMC Manager rubs her face between CantgetRite's neckline.

CantgetRite if finally enjoy a good day.

                    CANTGETRITE
    Oh, you're a freak.

CantgetRite grabs both of the AMC Manger's breasts roughly and the AMC Manger is loves it.

                    CANTGETRITE
    Dam girl.

AMC Manager playfully slaps CantgetRite in the face as he takes off his sunglasses and kisses her on her wrist, and continues to kiss her arm and

CantgetRite continues kissing her till

THEIR EYES MEET.

AMC Manager gets scared and screams.

CantgetRite screams.

A VERY TALL BLACK BLIND MAN enters the office and screams because he heard people screaming as he enters the office.

EXT. AMC THEATERS - MOMENTS LATER

CantgetRite walks up to Grant.

In almost an agreement knowing spiritually, CantgetRite extends the dollar bill as Grant grabs it with a sense of pride.

Grant's phone rings:

ABOB CALLING

6

STAY THE COURSE — chapter

INT. ABOB'S CAR - MOVING - AFTERNOON

ABOB 35, a handsome, distinguished Indian man dressed in a three-piece suit, speeds thru the streets.

Abob places his hand on Grant's shoulder

Grant is playing with a baseball in his hands.

                ABOB
        (breaking the silence)
Keep your head up. This is a good thing.

GRANT
How the hell is being blind and not able to hold a job a good thing?

ABOB
See. That right there is your problem.

GRANT
Getting my eyes yanked out is a good thing!

ABOB
Everything happens for a reason. Don't question it. Trust it.

GRANT
(snickers)
Easy for you to say. You pretty much have the life ever since we were fifth-teen.

Abob cuts off two drivers.

ABOB
Happiness is a choice. A choice I made for myself years ago. Every day I wanted to kill that man that killed my parents. Everyday. And it got to the point where it was affecting my life and everyone around me. I was becoming someone that I didn't recognize. Once I learned to let go. All that tension, all that hatred, all the negativity. All of it went away.

GRANT
(sarcasm)
That easy.

ABOB
Took me six years. Focus on the now. Go outside and start learning to breathe with the wind, talk to the wind, connect with nature. Stop focusing on things you can't control, like the past. Focus on things you can handle. Yourself. And until you don't and if you don't move forward...you will always be stuck between two doors.

Abob takes both hands off the steering wheel while driving 80 mph

Abob turns over one of his palms up.

ABOB
A door that closed and a

Abob turns his other palm up.

ABOB
A door that just opened. If you stay still. You will never walk down the path of enlightenment and discover your true calling.

Abob grabs the wheel and cuts off 3 drivers on the highway.

GRANT
(sarcasm)
Learning brail was always on my bucket list.

Abob cuts across three lanes.

ABOB
Yes. That's the spirit. Positivity. Positivity.

Abob pulls out a VAPE PEN and places it in Grant's pocket.

ABOB
(continue)
Here's a little something to help.

Grant pulls the vape pen and hands it back.

Abob grabs the vape pen and places it back in Grant's pocket. Abob pats the pocket.

ABOB
Enjoy it. At least you no longer married to that up-tight Mormon what's her face.

GRANT
Suzy

ABOB
And your son, Bingbong, is a fantastic chef. That soufflé is breathtaking.

Abob tabs Grant's pocket.

ABOB
That helped me not go batshit crazy. Let's grab some pizza, beers, and weed to welcome your new dog.

GRANT
You're not going to disappear on me again?

Abob parks his car.

ABOB
I promise. Sorry for last time, I had over time. I'll make it up to you with some ice cream tonight.

Abob's CELLPHONE RINGS

                      ABOB
I won't disappear

Answering his phone call.

             COMPUTER VOICE
Lawful.

Grant opens the door and extends his hand out.

                  GRANT
Going to need some help.
        (beat)
Abob?

Abob has disappeared.

Grant closes the door and pulls out the vape pen.

                  GRANT
     (snaps his fingers)
OK.

Grant starts breathing exercises.

                  GRANT
Learn to let go, Grant. Learn to let go. You can do this. You can

Grant takes a deep breath.

                  GRANT
This is so fucking stupid.

Grant takes a big puff from the vape pen.

                  GRANT
I hope he's getting his ass kicked.

7

Chapter
DESTINY
HISTORY
SAVIOR

INT. UNDERGROUND FIGHT ARENA - NIGHT

SERIOUS OF SHOTS

A) Fighter #4 has Donna in a headlock while Fighter #5 and Fighter #6 are taking turns kicking Dan in the groin.

B) Dan laughs, lifts up his dress, taunting both fighters to kick him harder in the groin.

C) Dan choke-slams Fighter #5 with his 36DD breast.

D) Dan punches Fighter #6 with his 36DD breast multiple times.

D) Dan jumps off the ropes making his signature final move on Fighter #6

BACK TO SCENE:

INT. UNDERGROUND FIGHT ARENA - NIGHT

Blood is everywhere.

Kemosabe's white hoodie turned into a RED HOODIE hoodie robe because of the BLOOD.

                FIGHT ANNOUNCER (O.S.)
     The winner and still undefeated. Donna, the man-
     titty.

                      DONNA
     What should I do?

                    KEMOSABE
     Fulfill your destiny. Teach the one of the one of
     the one being the one of the ones.

                      DONNA
     Do you think my son will forgive me?

Fighter #1 and Fighter #6 both rush towards Kemosabe.

Kemosabe knocks out both fighters with just one slap.

CU - DONNA

Kemosabe holds Donna's bloody chin.

                    KEMOSABE
     He will because he's the spitting image of you. An
     archer.

                    DONNA

My son?

EXT. TIP OF MOUNT FUJI - NIGHT

Kemosabe starts to tell the story of The Blind Archer.

We see a MAN fall from the sky, landing with the help of the winds.

The winds become a protective shield around this MAN who has a quiver holding arrows while he's holding a bow in one hand and an arrow in the other.

Thunder and lighting light up the sky which helps to show off this Man's archery attire who has a head-ban covering his eyes.

                    KEMOSABE (O.S.)
          For every generation, a blind archer is born. This
          archer will be our savor of this planet against the
          forces beyond these worlds. The blind archer
          must first learn how to control the winds of nature
          if we shaw have a fighting chance against these
          dark forces. For then will this blind archer be able
          to see and become the guardian of this world.

                    DONNA (O.S.)
Grant?

This mystery man aligns the arrow and shoots at the camera.

                    DONNA
          But, I owe The Crypto gang money.

                    KEMOSABE
          You're afraid of Doge and Shiba?

Donna shows fear in her face.

                    KEMOSABE
          You literally kicked 6 guys asses and you're afraid
          of those two?

                    GRANT
          I counted 8 Master Kemosabe.

Kemosabe slaps Donna's face continuously.

DONNA'S POV

Kemosabe's hand back and forth.

                                        FADE TO BLACK

55

EXT. ANIMAL SHELTER PARKING LOT - DAY

GRANT'S POV

PITCH DARKNESS

All we hear is Grant stumbling, falling, and bumping into unknown objects.

BACK TO SCENE:

CU - GRANT

Grant's face has a couple of bumps and scratches due to trying to walk 60 feet from Abob's car to the Animal Shelter's entrance.

INT. ANIMAL SHELTER - DAY

CINDY YUMI, 35 Japanese women, gives Grant a dog-leash connecting to an obedient GERMAN SHEPHERD.

CINDY
Wait right here while I get the release form.

LAPORSHA is a West Highland White Terrier with a BLACK FEMALE HUMAN HEAD superimposed onto the dog's body.

LaPorsha, the only dog left in the shelter, walks up to the cage.

LAPORSHA
Oh, for fuck sake. You're picking the German over

LaPorsha shows off her dog body.

LAPORSHA (CONTINUOUS)
This black beauty?

GRANT
Who's there?

> LAPORSHA
> Fuckin' bullshit, wait. You can hear me?

> GRANT
> I'm blind, not deaf.

Grant pulls out the vape and smells it.

> LAPORSHA
> You ain't hallucinating Nigga! Give me the vape.

Grant extends the vape.

LaPorsha is staring at the camera.

LaPorsha opens up the cage, grabs Grant's vape, starts smoking.

> LAPORSHA
> If you are seriously thinking. How the hell is her face.

Laporsha poses her HUMAN BLACK FEMALE FACE.

> LAPORSHA (CONTINUOUS)
> Stuck on that little dog's body.

LaPorsha poses her LITTLE DOG BODY.

> LAPORSHA (CONTINUOUS)
> And she can talk to that guy
> (points at Grant)
> Then Nigga, you pick the wrong fucking movie.
> And I ain't yo bitch.

LaPorsha snorts a line of cocaine.

LAPORSHA
Nope, this shit might be fucking entertaining your broke ass but, this here is real to me. One hundred. Either that or this stuff

LaPorsha vapes.

              LAPORSHA
Is this fucking laced?.

LaPorsha walks back into the cage and locks herself in.

              LAPORSHA
              (towards Grant)
Do you think that German is going to help you?

              GRANT
Well technically you are a bitch. Female dog and any help, helps me.

              LAPORSHA
I would say something but, my granddaddy told me never to make fun of a cripple, just get me out of this place, and I'll be your seeing-eye dog.

              GRANT
And how exactly are you going to help? And if you aren't a bitch. I ain't your cripple.

LaPorsha grabs Grant's cellphone.

              LAPORSHA
Lets find out Mr.

GRANT'S CELLPHONE SCREEN

A wedding photo of Grant and his pregnant wife, SUZY

BACK TO SCENE:

LAPORSHA
Well, first of all, who's the broad in your screen savor

GRANT
My ex-wife Suzy

LAPORSHA
Ok, that's just sad. First, what the fuck? Why do you still have this as your screen especially being single and hello? Blind!

LaPorsha takes a photo of Grant and replaces the screensaver.

LAPORSHA
And what's better than a seeing-eye dog? How about one that is telling you exactly what everyone around you is doing. Let me be your eyes.

GRANT
My name is Grant.

LAPORSHA
LaPorsha. I hope you have more weed.

Cindy returns with paperwork.

GRANT
I change my mind.
    (points at LaPorsha)
I would like that dog.

Cindy gets startled by the odd change.

LaPorsha drinks her whiskey while she's looking at Cindy's body language.

                    CINDY
Are you sure? The female west highland terrier came in yesterday and appears to have had several drugs in her system. She's defiantly been abused by her owners.

                    LAPORSHA
Self abused.

LaPorsha snorts a line of cocaine.

                    LAPORSHA
And I know you've been checking out my man. Here's just a taste Grant on how helpful I can be for you. Repeat after me.

                    CINDY
She will need constant attention after the drugs leave her

                    LAPORSHA
Weed, Whiskey, weed, more weed. Weed.

                    CINDY
    (continue)
System and she will be very moody.

                  LAPORSHA
Can you shut her up... weed. Ugh. Speed up and repeat after me.

                    CINDY
It's a forever home.

LAPORSHA

I am sure
   (beat)
If I'm wrong, I'll bring back the wonderful LaPorsha this Friday and take you to dinner after, but if i'm happy with sexy yours truly LaPorsha, what time would our dinner date be

GRANT

I am sure
   (beat)
If I'm wrong, I'll bring back her this Friday and take you to dinner after, but if i'm happy with you sexy yours truly what time would our dinner date be

Cindy blushes as she picks up LaPorscha and hands her to Grant.

Cindy blushes as she picks up LaPorscha and hands her to Grant.

LAPORSHA

Oh fuck me, she smells good. She smells like a stripper.

LaPorsha licks Cindy's neck.

LAPORSHA

She tastes good too.

Smells Grant.

LAPORSHA

You could use some help.

Cindy grabs her cellphone and taps Grants cell phone. She sees

GRANT'S CELLPHONE

The screen lights up, showing a photo of Grant from the floor's POV - Cindy smiles.

CINDY YUMI'S CONTACT NOTIFICATION APPEARS

LaPorsha is grabbing the cellphone.

                    LAPORSHA (O.S.)
            (pronouncing Cindy's last name)
    Cindy Use me

                    CINDY
    6 pm

EXT. ANIMAL SHELTER PARKING LOT

LaPorsha immediately takes off the leash and starts vaping.

                    LAPORSHA
    Freedom bitches!

LaPorsha vapes again.

                    LAPORSHA
    Where's your car.

                    GRANT
    I'm blind, remember.

LAPORSHA
No shit, please don't tell me that you walked. Are you sure your name isn't Lincoln?

Laporsha grabs Grant's cell phone.

                    LAPORSHA
        Uber or Lyft

Grant unsuccessfully tries to grab his phone back.

                    GRANT
        No.

                    LAPORSHA
        How did you get here?

Grant pulls out car keys.

                    GRANT
        A friend of mine took me.

LaPorsha grabs the keys and locates Abob's TESLA

                    GRANT
        I can't drive! Going to ask Cindy if

LaPorsha jumps onto Grant and slaps him.

                    LAPORSHA
Don't get cocky motherfucker... you don't want to sound like a cripple do you? You can use the pedal while I'll steer.

LaPorsha vapes and places it on Grants' lips.

                    LAPORSHA
        Teamwork.

LaPorsha raises her paw and immediately remembers Grant is blind as she retracts her paw and pours herself another whiskey while toasting herself.

9

Chapter
DRIVING WHILE BLIND

EXT. JUNCTION 5 FREEWAY VERMONT - DAY

Abob's car speeds down the highway cutting off multiple drivers.

Grant and LaPorsha swerving on the freeway and cuts off a police vehicle.

INT. ABOB'S CAR - MOVING

Grant is sitting in the driver's seat while LaPorsha is steering.

                LAPORSHA
    Give it more gas captain.

Police lights and sirens behind Grant and LaPorsha.

                GRANT
    Are the cops pulling us over?

LAPORSHA
    Yeah, don't worry. Use your white card.

                    GRANT
    Don't be racist.

Grant and LaPorsha pullover

INT. ABOB'S CAR - DAY

POLICE OFFICER STERLING walks towards the driver's seat.

                    LAPORSHA
    How's that racist.

                    GRANT
    Would you quit and help? How am I going to
    explain driving blindfold?

Police knock on the window.

                    LAPORSHA
    Just makeup something. Just make sure he
    doesn't pet me.

Grant rolls down the window.

                    GRANT
    Hello Mr. Officer

                    OFFICER STERLING
    Are you blind?

                    GRANT
    No, This

Grant touches and adjust his eye cloth covering.

GRANT
It's the all new high-tech eyewear 6000 that helps with navigation and car steering.

OFFICER STERLING
Bullshit! How many fingers am I holding?

LAPORSHA
(towards Grant)
The dick isn't holding any fingers.

GRANT
Trick question since you aren't holding any fingers Officer.

Officer holds out three fingers.

LAPORSHA
He's now holding three.

GRANT
Three

Officer Sterling changes his fingers to six

LAPORSHA
Six.

GRANT
Six.

Officer Sterling inspects Grant's eye cover headband.

OFFICER STERLING
That's just amazing.

GRANT
Yeah, those Chinese are coming up with fantastic techs.

Officer Sterling makes a double finger point gesture.

LAPORSHA
Oh, he's doing that white finger-pointing shit.

Grant returns the double finger-pointing.

OFFICER STERLING
Amazing. You really aren't blind.

GRANT
No. I apologize. I must have been swirling.

OFFICER STERLING
You did cut me off back at the over the path.

GRANT
I didn't mean to, Officer. I was rushing home before the NyQuil I took for my cold kicks in.
(fakes yawn)
But, really, I'm blind, and my talking weed-smoking dog was driving this whole time.

LAPORSHA DOES THE FINGER GESTURE

Grant and Officer Sterling's finger gesture each other.

Both Grant and Officer Sterling start to laugh.

OFFICER STERLING
Well, try to drive a little slower next time.

OFFICER STERLING
Amazing China people technology.

LaPorsha rolls a blunt while shaking her head.

                    LAPORSHA
        Fucking white people.

10

RUBEE Chapter

INT. GRANT'S TRAILER - NIGHT

Knock on the door.

Bingbong answers

>   DONNA
>   Hello son.

>   BINGBONG
>   Hi grandpa.

>   DONNA
>   (correcting Bingbong)
>   It's grandma.

Bingbong gestures to Donna to come closer.

Bingbong whispers in Donna's ear.

>   BINGBONG
>   I may be a child, but I'm not blind and stupid.
>   (sadistic)
>   Don.

Bingbong hands Donna a bucket of homemade chicken and continues to work in the kitchen and on his website, ignoring everyone.

RUBEE, an elderly woman in an electric wheelchair, rolls up to Donna.

                    RUBEE
Well, look what the cat dragged in.

                    DONNA
Hi Momma.

                    RUBEE
Don't you momma me. You left us.

                    DONNA
I had to.

                    RUBEE
I told you but, you don't listen. I told you that I didn't want to take your bet.

                    DONNA
It was a sure thing.

                    RUBEE
And look what a sure thing you are now.

                    DONNA
If I didn't leave, they were threatening to kill me.

                    RUBEE
Do you think putting on a fake wig and some fake boobies will hide your identity?

                    DONNA
Well.

RUBEE
Well, ever since you left, I had to incur your debt, and you still owe 25k, and you came back to enter the tournament again. Might I remind you that you're still banned for life ever since that fiasco?

DONNA
Well.

RUBEE
Well, if you came back to visit. It was nice seeing you but, I would leave before Grant shows up since he wouldn't be happy to see your face.

DONNA
That's why I came back.

RUBEE
What can you possibly do to make things right?

DONNA
Train him.

RUBEE
His mother left him. You left him, and then Suzy left him. Train him? For what? The left-O'lympics.

DONNA
Archery competition.

RUBEE
Excuse my French. Are you on fucking drugs?

DONNA
No. I'm serious.

RUBEE

Archery?

DONNA
Archery?

RUBEE
I guess it's true what they say when a man loses his marbles, he loses his manhood.

DONNA
Mom, He's the one.

Rubee does a 360 on her electric wheelchair.

RUBEE
(towards Bingbong)
Grant is going to be an Archer.

Bingbong jumps on the kitchen island counter and pulls back on an imaginary bow and arrow.

Rubee stands up and tries to doge an imaginary arrow from Bingbong.

Bingbong releases an imaginary arrow.

Rubee pretends to get shot in the back by the imaginary arrow and drops to the floor laughing.

Bingbong starts to laugh louder, causing Rubee to laugh even louder.

Rubee is laughing on the floor.

RUBEE
My grandson is going to become the blind archer!

DONNA
I'm serious, mom. Master Kemosabe.

RUBEE
(laughing)
The next thing you tell me is that Grant becomes our only hope for survival when an alien spaceship invades earth.

BINGBONG
I come shoot in peace.

Rubee jumps back into her electric wheelchair, does a 360 while imaginary shooting an arrow at Bingbong.

Both Rubee and Bingbong continue to laugh together.

RUBEE
(towards Donna)
You're funny.

11

INT. CINDY'S APARTMENT - EVENING

Cindy is talking to ACHILLES, her Pit-bull, while changing and getting ready for her night job.

                    CINDY
     I met someone today, and no, not from my night
     job.

Jumping out of the shower.

                    CINDY
     You're right; he better not be a cheater. This one
     feels different.

Cindy's phone rings.

82

A photo of a man wearing an NBA REFEREE with his face scratched off and the name: Cheating Asshole Cheater appears on the screen.

                    CINDY
              (towards the phone)
         Cheater!

Cindy hugs and kisses Achilles while grabbing her purse.

                    CINDY
         Dinner is next to the frig, and I left the TV on for
         you. Who's my sexy beast. My sexy beast. You're
         always right. Hope he's not a criminal either.

Achilles loves the attention as Cindy walks out of her apartment.

Achilles jumps onto the couch and starts watching Television.

INT. ABOB'S CAR - DAY

Police Officer Sterling gets in his patrol car and drives off.

LaPorsha takes a huge bong hit.

                    LAPORSHA
         You lucky son of a bitch. I can't believe you got off
         with a warning. Let's try this again and this time,
         try not to have a lead foot.

INT. ABOB'S CAR - MOVING

                    GRANT
         Have we exited Green Valley?

LAPORSHA

No.

GRANT

Where are you heading?

LAPORSHA

After sitting on your lap for so long, I need to take you somewhere first.

GRANT

Where?

12

INT. JIGGLY JIGGLY - NIGHT

A semi-decent gentleman's club.

Grant is getting a lap dance from STRIPPER COFFEE, 25 Carmelo chocolate skin black woman with Afro.

                    STRIPPER COFFEE
    You feel ready to stick your finger in my coffee.

                    GRANT
            Why the name Coffee?

LAPORSHA
        Stop trying to play twenty questions.

                     GRANT
                (towards LaPorsha)
           What are we doing at a strip club?

                 STRIPPER COFFEE
                 (grinding harder)
         Having some good o'fashion black coffee.

Grant moans in pleasure.

                 STRIPPER COFFEE
           Do you always talk to your dog?

                     GRANT
                 Just started.

Stripper Coffee touches Grants eyewear.

                 STRIPPER COFFEE
              Is it really that bad?

Grant readjust his eye band.

                 STRIPPER COFFEE
                 (whisper in-ear)
           Thank you for the dance love.

Suzy brings Grant a soda.

                      SUZY
                 Six dollars.
                      (beat)
           Grant? What are you doing here!

GRANT
Suzy?

LAPORSHA
Oh, drama. Fucking love it.

GRANT
Well?

SUZY
None of your fucking business!

GRANT
Business? You left me with a baby.

SUZY
I wasn't going to be the only one to take responsibility.

GRANT
Yeah, that's why they call it marriage! For two people too.
            (frustrated)
Never mind

SUZY
What do you want?

GRANT
Defiantly don't want to be here

SUZY
Good. Leave. Loser.

GRANT
Loser?

LAPORSHA
Lets go.

SUZY
You're a loser just like your daddy, and I wasn't going to be stuck living in a trailer with you.

GRANT
It was for one year so that I could play ball.

SUZY
Sure. Brooklyn was never there for you anyways. One year my ass.

LAPORSHA
Let go.

GRANT
You sound just as bitchy as ever.
　　(beat)
Suzy.

LAPORSHA
Lets go

SUZY
Well, it's a two-drink minimum. Either pay now or leave. Or you still a broke ass.

BACKSTAGE - CONTINUOUS

Cindy is applying last-minute makeup and adjusting her outfit as other STRIPPERS come by to hug and kiss for support.

Cindy grabs a perfume called: "Smell like a stripper" and sprays all over her body.

Cindy walks out onto the stage.

INT. JIGGY JIGGY - CONTINUOUS

STRIPPER DJ (O.S.)
Ok, fellas, give a warm welcome to our next dancer that graces us from the East. Saki-Saki

Techno mixed with hip-hop fills the stage.

Cindy Yumi, dressed like a slutty schoolgirl, starts dancing and showing off her sexy back.

LaPorsha drops her drink in surprise.

LAPORSHA
It's time to go. Lets go!

LaPorsha is jumping on Grants' lap.

LAPORSHA
You won't be poking me for a while now.

GRANT
Ok, ok, ok.

Suzy points to the backdoor exit.

Cindy Yumi gives the audience a view of her firm tone body.

CINDY'S POV

Multiple men are throwing money at Cindy.

A man is exiting the backdoor.

ADAM GARDENA, 51, drooling with a smile on his face.

BACK TO SCENE

PRIVATE ROOM

Cindy is giving a private lap dance to Adam Gardena.

                    CINDY
        Why so far babe.

                    ADAM GARDENA
        Work.

Rubbing her ass in his face.

                    CINDY
        Going to miss you.

                    CINDY
        One day a girl is going to fall out of the sky and steal you away from everyone.

Adam adjust himself as Cindy rides Adam

                    CINDY
            (Whispering)
        Will miss you.

13

FAKIN' MOMMY

INT. GRANT'S TRAILER - NIGHT

Donna and Rubee are enjoying Bingbong's chicken as Grand and LaPorsha enter.

>   BINGBONG
>   Dog!

Bingbong runs over and grabs LaPorsha.

>   LAPORSHA
>   Weed, watermelon, and chicken. I'm starting to
>   like this place.

>   GRANT
>   Who's here.

Donna trying to find the courage to talk.

Rubee jumps out of her wheelchair and pushes Donna out the door.

>   RUBEE
>   We'll be right back

EXT. GRANT'S TRAILER - NIGHT

>   RUBEE
>   What are you doing!

>   DONNA
>   Pretending to be his mother.

>   RUBEE
>   Don. You're his father, no matter what you
>   stupidly did.

>   DONNA
>   I can't. If they find out. They will kill us.

>   RUBEE
>   No, they won't. They want their monies just like
>   me. They don't give a shit about you.

>   DONNA
>   I know.

>   RUBEE
>   Don't ruin that boy's life with your mistake.

>   DONNA
>   I'm trying not to.

>   RUBEE

His mother left him the moment he was born, and his so-called father left him the moment he lost his eyes. You don't think for once he's been through enough.

                    DONNA

I can't

                    RUBEE

Well, I won't be there to rescue you like I did last time.

                    DONNA

What last time.

Rubee drags Donna back inside

INT. GRANT'S TRAILER - CONTINUOUS

                    LAPORSHA

When am I going to get a half-acre and a mule?

                    RUBEE

You know what. Whatever you want to do. It's your choice. You always seem to have all the answers now. Do you.

                    DONNA

I'm trying to make things right.

                    RUBEE

Trying is your first mistake.

Rubee kisses Grant goodbye and jumps into her mobile wheelchair.

Rubee drives up to Bingbong, who is holding LaPorsha.

                    RUBEE
Such a cute doggie

Rubee drives off.

                    DONNA
Hi Son

                    GRANT
Mom?

                    DONNA
Yes

                    LAPORSHA
              (whispering to herself)
That's one ugly ass mother.

Bingbong is feeding LaPorsha chicken and waffles while petting her.

                    BINGBONG
That's not his mother.

Bingbong logs onto

YOUTUBE

Bingbong clicks on a video showing Don "Bullseye" Davis shooting his arrow into the audience, and the arrow freakish makes a left from the gust of wind and plucks out Grant's eyes and killing an American Eagle right after.

LaPorsha's paw clicks on replay.

GRANT
(hearing the youtube)
Stoping playing that video.

Grant, out of anger, grabs a BANANA off the kitchen counter and throws it at Donna's face.

Donna catches it.

DONNA (V.O.)
How will I know if he really is the one?

KEMOSABE (V.O.)
You will know. It's an undeniable feeling.

Donna stares at the banana he caught that was just inches from hitting him straight in the face.

14

TRAINING REVEAL Chapter

EXT. VERMONT MOUNTAIN - MORNING

Grant, Donna, and LaPorsha are in open farmland.

Donna gives Grant his legendary bow.

          GRANT
     (sarcasm)
We really are doing this.

          DONNA
Yes

          GRANT
You came back into my life after so many years to teach me Archery? This is my dad's sport.

          DONNA
I'm the one who taught your father everything he knows.

          GRANT
You left my father the moment I was born.

DONNA
Yeah... I'm sorry about that.

GRANT
So you think, fuck it. Blindman, maybe he can be the Ray Charles of Archery, and yet you're sorry.

DONNA
You have to believe what I tell you. You are the chosen one.

GRANT
Chosen for what?

DONNA
Being the chosen one comes with great responsibility.

Donna puts on a quiver with a couple of arrows for Grant.

LaPorsha jumps into Grant's quiver and pulls out a Whiskey bottle.

LAPORSHA
I like it in here!

LaPorsha takes out a bong from the quiver and starts to smoke.

LAPORSHA
There's something you need to know.

GRANT
I'm not an archer.

DONNA
You're not a baseball pitcher either.

                      GRANT
          (Anger)
    Dad?

                    LAPORSHA
    Donna isn't your mother. She's your father.

Grant starts pulling out an Arrow and shooting each arrow at Donna missing each time.

LaPorsha is giving Grant direction.

                    LAPORSHA
        Higher.

Grant misses

                    LAPORSHA
        Lower a little

The arrow misses Donna.

                    LAPORSHA
        3 o'clock.

The arrow misses Donna by inches.

                     DONNA
        Yes, you're getting it.

                    LAPORSHA
        A little higher towards 2 o'clock

                     DONNA
        Channel, it, son.

Grant pulls out the last arrow from his quiver and shoots it towards Donna.

The arrow flies right at Donna's face.

Donna catches the arrow.

                    DONNA
          Now you're feeling it.

                    GRANT
          Feeling what! I can't see because of you!

Grant exhausted and panting after shooting multiple arrows one after another.

Donna walks up to Grant and places the Arrow he caught in Grant's hand.

                    DONNA
          Now turn around, take a deep breath

Grant aligns the arrow turns around.

                    DONNA
          Listen to the air, hear the leaves, feel the wind.
          Use your other senses besides your sight.

Grant listens to the wind and aims the arrow.

                    LAPORSHA
          Aim it at your 9 o'clock.

Grant adjusts his aim and releases the arrow.

WHISKEY SHOT

EXT. BOSTON ARCHERY COMPETITION - AFTERNOON

Hundreds of Archers compete in the 1st round Archery qualification competition.

The arrow misses the target completely.

LaPorsha, standing inside Grant's quiver, passes Grant the arrow giving directions while vaping.

                    LAPORSHA
     If you keep missing, we will lose.

                    GRANT
  I feel pathetic.
        (sarcasm)
  The chosen one.

LaPorsha places the vape in Grant's mouth.

                    LAPORSHA
        Ah, shut up, relax and listen to me.

Grant takes a big hit.

                    GRANT
        This is the 6th time missing. If I don't make the
        next four, I'm not moving on to the next round.

LaPorsha pours a shot glass of Whiskey and pours it in Grant's mouth as he pulls back on another arrow.

                    LAPORSHA
        You need this. You're way too uptight.

LaPorsha pours another shot of Whiskey and pours it in Grant's mouth again.

                    GRANT
        I can't no more.

                    LAPORSHA
        Yes, you can. If I had a snicker, I shove it up your
        ass.

Grant starts coughing, and his fingers on the arrow slip.

LaPorsha's eyes widen.

Grant hits a bullseye.

                    ANNOUNCER (O.S.)
        Grant's first point after missing the last four puts
        him back in the running.

DONNA
That's my son.
(yelling to Grant)
You can do it, Son!

LAPORSHA
Wow, that's impressive.

GRANT
Oh, now you're impressed?

LAPORSHA
Are you kidding? Lets go play by play. You're blind.

Grant grabs the arrow from LaPorsha.

LAPORSHA
You're intoxicated, and might I add less bitchy thanks to yours truly.

Grant pulls back on the arrow wobbly.

LAPORSHA
We're both defiantly high.

Grant aims to the sky.

LAPORSHA
No! Not that high freak. Lower. Lower. Lower!

LaPorsha grabs Grants by both ears from the back and helps Grant aim.

LAPORSHA
Now.

Grant hits the target inches away from another bullseye.

                    LAPORSHA
We're getting better at this.

                    ANNOUNCER (O.S.)
If Grant can continue putting points on the board, he will continue to advance to the second round. Grant Davis may be in last place but, he's also blind folks. An archer that is blind. No one ever saw that coming for sure.

Grant pulls back and hits the target again, inches away from bullseye.

                    ANNOUNCER (O.S.)
It looks like Grant Davis qualifies for the second round next week.

DIGITAL SCOREBOARD

Davis' name is in last place, and his name is the last person to qualify for round two.

Grant and LaPorsha high-five each other missing each other's high-five.

Donna is the loudest clapper in the stand.

                    DONNA
That's my boy!

LaPorsha takes a bow while smoking a bong.

Chapter MICKEY D'S 100K AND COCAINE!

INT. MCDONALD'S - DAY

LaPorsha, Grant, and Donna all are at McDonald sharing a meal.

LaPorsha is pouring some whiskey into her McDonald's cup and Grant's cup.

Donna steals Grant's fries

                DONNA
    It's a 100k grand prize this year in the finals.

LaPorsha stops what she is doing and starts to pay more attention.

                GRANT
    That's nice.

                DONNA
    That would solve all our problems.

LaPorsha snorts a line of cocaine while saying

                LAPORSHA
    Nothing like Cocaine and MickeyD's. It's the Breakfast of Champions!

                GRANT
    I'm not an archer.

                LAPORSHA
    Muthafucka, for 100k. Shit. Yes... you are.

                DONNA
    Yes, you are.

                GRANT
    I just got lucky.

DONNA
You were able to make it past the first round.

LAPORSHA
That wasn't luck.

GRANT
Luck.

DONNA
You got the gift, son.

LAPORSHA (she coaxes)
Yeah you right, that was a fucking miracle. No fucking way you can do that shit again.

GRANT
I will be going up against top archers in the next round, then what.

DONNA
And they will be going up against the one.

GRANT
Stop saying that.

DONNA
Believe it, son.

GRANT
Winning that kind of money would be a godsend.

DONNA
You're just two more rounds away.

GRANT
If I did win, half the money is already gone.

DONNA
I know a doctor that can do miracles for half the budget. I bet he can help.

GRANT
Bingbong already found me a doctor but, it'll cost 25k.

DONNA
Well, there you go, so don't give up. You did great last round.

GRANT
I don't think so, and besides, I don't have the money to pay for the competition entrance fee.

DONNA
Well, too bad, I already signed you up, and it's paid.

Grant pulls out a vape and smokes inside McDonalds.

LAPORSHA
Pass that shit, homie.

Grant passes the vape to LaPorsha.

DONNA
I got paid from my last gig because I believe in you, so don't throw away this gift.

GRANT
Well, it's your money, so don't blame me if I lost your $5,000 gift.

DONNA
Let me keep training you, so stay by my side.

GRANT
Like you just left me, and mom did?

DONNA
I had to. Don't follow in my foot's steps.

GRANT
That won't be a problem. Who am I going to leave?

LaPorsha smokes a cigarette and flings it at the wall while looking at Grant.

DONNA
They were after me, and I had to leave, or they would have killed you and me.

Donna starts to tell the story to Grant of why he had to disappear.

DONNA'S FLASHBACK

EXT. VERMONT STATE FAIR - DAY

Don "BULLSEYE" Davis pulls out an arrow and taps Bluetooth.

DON "BULLSEYE" DAVIS
Call Mamma.

INT. RUBEE'S BOOKIE OFFICE - DAY

Rubee is looking at multiple computer monitors, all showing Vegas betting points.

Rubee's cellphone rings.

DON "BULLSEYE" DAVIS
Mama... double the wager with those Vegas people you talk to on the computer.

RUBEE
You don't have the money, and Vegas points don't look good if you lose.

DON "BULLSEYE" DAVIS
Loan it to me, Mama. I'm guaranteed to win.

RUBEE
You don't understand if you put that much money and you bet on the sure thing. Vegas has a way of manipulating the game. Vegas always wins.

DON "Bullseye" Davis pulls back on his bow.

DON "BULLSEYE" DAVIS
But, Mama... we can triple our money, and we be set for life. Me you, Grant and Bingbong. How can Vegas manipulate Archery competition? I'm good for it.

Don releases the arrow.

RUBEE
You don't even have 30k to cover your cost. You are asking for a 20k loan, and on top of that, you're only going to win 10k. Too much of a gamble, son.

The Arrow hits the bullseye.

DON "BULLSEYE" DAVIS
(Releases the arrow)
I'm a sure thing. 7th time Champion, here I come.

Arrow hits the bullseye. The crowd goes wild.

                    RUBEE
This doesn't feel right. It's June 6, and you're 6x world champion.

                    DON "BULLSEYE" DAVIS
Stop with the sixes superstition, Mama! We can finally triple our monies with this hear Dogecoin winnings because I'm Bullseye!

                    RUBEE
Cryptocurrency is very volatile. You have better luck fighting against six cage fighters. OK. I pray that you know what you're doing.

                    RUBEE
You better win. Vegas doesn't like losing either, and Crypto are run by mobsters.

Rubee starts to input Don's bet on the Vegas system Computer.

RUBEE'S CELLPHONE: VEGAS CALLING

Rubee grabs the cellphone and is hesitant to accept it.

                                    END OF
                                    FLASHBACK

                                    BACK TO SCENE:

INT. MCDONALDS - DAY

                    GRANT
You expect me to believe that?

DONNA
It's the truth.

GRANT
Her breast didn't knock you out.

LAPORSHA
I bet she's great at parties.

DONNA
All I can tell you is what happened.

GRANT
Not what I saw last time.

17

Chapter
TUNE IN TOKYO! COME IN TOKYO!

INT. DEBBIE DOGERS - NIGHT

Grant, LaPorsha, and Cindy all sit in a booth at Debbie Dogers, a semi-upscale restaurant serving nothing but upscale hot dogs and fries.

The waiter serves everyone a hotdog, fries, and soda.

                    LAPORSHA (V.O.)
     Goddam, there's a lot of eating in this movie.

LaPorsha snorts a line of cocaine on her hotdog.

                    LAPORSHA
     Nothing like snorting cocaine on a weenie.

                    CINDY
     Congratulations, I heard that you advanced to the second round.

                    LAPORSHA
     Someone's a stalker.

                    CINDY
     I have to ask.

                    LAPORSHA
     Yes, you can have his D.

                    GRANT
     Let me guess. How can I shoot an arrow while being blind?

Cindy nods yes while eating the hotdog seductively.

Grant grabs the dog.

> GRANT
> This little girl is my eyes, and she tells me where to shoot the arrow.

LaPorsha laughs nervously.

> LAPORSHA
> I guess you ain't getting the D tonight.

> LAPORSHA
> Shut up and just repeat. You need to get laid badly. You hold on to the arrow too tight.

> CINDY
> Wow, that's amazing. What are your plans for the winnings?

> GRANT
> Have to win first

Cindy touches Grant's hand.

> LAPORSHA
> She defiantly wants the D. Touch her hand, you idiot. Smile. And stop looking towards me.

Grant touches Cindy's hand.

> GRANT
> Well, it'll help pay for eye transplant surgery. It's pretty much the only reason why I decided to enter. It'll be blind luck.

CINDY
          You're an archer by blood.
                    (beat)
          I bet you know how to hit the right spot.

                    LAPORSHA
          Oh, she defiantly going to get the D.

                    CINDY
          Look on the bright side. If you lose, I'll go
          stripping at the club so I can help.

                    LAPORSHA
          Oh, I know you would, honey!

Grant chuckles nervously.

LaPorsha grabs Grant by the collar.

                    CINDY
          Ah, she does love you.

                    LAPORSHA
          Ask her if she wants to hold me... woman loves
          this shit.

                    GRANT
          Wanna hold her.

Cindy's eyes light up as Grant places LaPorsha in her arms.

                    LAPORSHA
          I feel like you need to move in.

LaPorsha grabs Cindy's face with both paws and turns her face towards Grant.

                    LAPORSHA

> Go on and kiss the girl.

Grant goes in for a kiss but misses and lands a kiss on the tip of Cindy's chin.

Cindy returns the kiss by kissing Grant on the chin.

INT. CINDY'S APARTMENT - NIGHT

Achilles is sleeping upside down in Cindy's messy Apartment.

BEDROOM

Cindy starts to take off Grants EYE CLOTH COVER.

Grant stops Cindy.

                    CINDY
    Don't be ashamed.

Grant lowers his head.

Cindy lifts up Grant's face with finger while kissing Grant as she takes off his eye cloth cover.

Cindy is wearing nothing but a bra and is sitting on top of Grant, who is also nude.

Cindy takes off her bra.

                    CINDY
    Can you read brail?

Grant touches Cindy's breast.

CU - LAPORSHA LAYING AT THE EDGE OF THE BED

Cindy's pink bra lands on top of LaPorsha's head as she continues to drink her whiskey while smoking weed.

                    GRANT (O.S.)
          Tune in Tokyo! Come in Tokyo!

Both Grant and Cindy giggle as Cindy lets out a moan.

The bed starts to make LaPorsha slowly rise up and down as her eyes follow.

LaPorsha smiles as she finishes her whiskey.

LaPorsha walks passed Achilles who is sleeping upside down.

LaPorsha looks out the window and grabs Cindy's umbrella.

We can still hear Grant and Cindy having sex.

LaPorsha walks out of Cindy's Apartment.

18

EXT. NEIGHBORHOOD STREET - NIGHT

The Neighborhood looks like a 1952 era.

Everything on screen looks like it's filmed using Technicolor 3-Strip Camera

LAPORSHA'S MUSICAL NUMBER - DANCIN' IN COCAINE

LaPorsha starts to reenact the 1952 "Singin' In The Rain" scene.

It's not raining. It's flurrying snow. As it turns out, the flurries are cocaine falling from the sky.

LaPorsha extends her paw out from her umbrella, her whole hand and forearm are covered in cocaine.

LaPorsha is very surprised and is hesitant at first till she dabs her tongue on her paw for a taste.

LaPorsha's eyes light up, and her smile widens.

LaPorsha snorts all the cocaine off of her paw and forearms.

LaPorsha inverts her umbrella to catch as much cocaine from the sky.

Singin' In The Rain music starts to play.

LAPORSHA
(SINGING AND DANCE)

I'm dancin' in the rain just smokin' some endo a lot of endo in da rain.

What is this I feel? Is this cocaine and not snowy rain.

Oh, it's Cocaine oh, much better when it rains cocaine.

Lets snort a big line.

Lets snort a little line.

Snort till you can't find any more cocaine lines! Yes it is.

What it is? It's cocaine.

Oh, this makes me happy all the fucking time, every time.

My life is great with Grant, so I'll smoke in his name.

Glad he is getting laid because this rain is my cocaine.

I'm snorting, and I'm smokin', I'm dancing, I'm drinking because I am feeling happy in this cocaine snowy rain.

Because I'm dancin' in cocaine.

I'm dancin' in cocaine.

And I'm dancin' in cocaine.

My bitcoin is going up, and I'm no longer down in the cage because I snort a little cocaine all day, every day, even when I'm

Dancin'.

Dancin'.

Dancin' in cocaine!

Cocaine. Cocaine. Cocaine.

I finally found a forever home with Grant and Cocaine!

LAPORSHA'S MUSICAL NUMBER END

LaPorsha grabs as much cocaine off the ground and throws it up in the air.

Flood lights flash onto LaPorsha.

LaPorsha is covered from head to toe in cocaine.

Chapter

LET THAT BITCH FLY!

EXT. VERMONT FAIR GROUNDS - MORNING

SUPER: SEMI-FINALS ARCHERY CHAMPIONSHIP

Grant is pulling back and misses another shot. Grant is getting frustrated, calls dad.

Donna is watching from the stands with binoculars.

>DONNA
>It looks like you need to raise your arrow just a tab bit.

>GRANT
>I did, and I still keep getting three points.

>DONNA
>If you did have a talking dog, it should have been helping you.

>GRANT
>She's passed out.

>DONNA
>Because there's no such thing as a talking dog.

>GRANT
>(sarcasm)
>Oh... but a magical wind of nature will guild me to be the one.

DONNA
Yes. Our savor, The Blind Archer!

GRANT
Being blind and
(chuckles)
An archer does not make me the one. It fucking makes me still blind, shooting into the darkness.

Grant releases the arrow.

ANNOUNCER (O.S.)
Eight points for Grant Davis.

DONNA
Not bad, next time a tab bit left.

GRANT
Wake up LaPorsha. LaPorsha.

DONNA
There's no such thing as a talking dog.

Grant taps his blue tooth, hanging up on Donna

LAPORSHA
Where am I?

LaPorsha pours herself a shot of Whiskey.

GRANT
You're at the competition, and I'm losing. You're the only one that can see for me. Dam it. I'm going to lose, wake up!

LAPORSHA
Relax. I'm awake. Fuck. Not so loud.

                GRANT
Well... Stop drinking and doing cocaine, then.

              LAPORSHA
Chill. Fuck. Shit! Goddam. Didn't you just get laid. Fuck.

LaPorsha gives Grant better instructions.

              LAPORSHA
Higher. To the left more. Not so fast. Ok. Release the bitch.

Grant releases the arrow.

Grant lands nine points.

Grant pulls back on another arrow.

              LAPORSHA
Just a little more left. Let that bitch fly!

Grant releases the arrow.

The Arrow lands on the bullseye.

EXT. WINNER'S CIRCLE - MORNING

              MACK CHAZY
Here are your remaining Archers advancing to the finals.

There's a total of 25 Archers standing in the winner's circle.

LaPorsha snorts the last cocaine off her shoulders and passes out again in the quiver.

                    DONNA
        Wow, that was a close one.

                    GRANT
        Thanks.

Donna looks at LaPorsha passed out. Donna grabbing LaPorsha's paw

                    DONNA
        Nice to meet a talking dog.

Donna smithy waits for Grant's responds of any kind.

                    DONNA
                (voicing LaPorsha)
        Oh, hi, Mr. Archer... So so sorry I knocked out. I'm just so exhausted from all this chit-chat. Wheeze me.

                    GRANT
        Don't be a dick.

                    INGRID
        Did someone say dick?

INGRID, 30-year-old Swedish blondie with huge 36DDD breast walking towards Grant and Donna.

                    INGRID
                (toward Grant)
        I wanted to congratulate you on making it to the finals.

LaPorsha's and Donna's eyes widen as they both stares into Ingrid's huge 36DDD.

                    LAPORSHA
WOW, loo...

DONNA'S FLASHBACK

Ingrid walks towards Don "Bullseye" Davis and takes off her shirt.

                    LAPORSHA (V.O.)
          Look at those knockers!

Ingrid's left breast punches Don while Ingrid's right breast uppercuts Don's face.

Don release the arrow.

                              FLASHBACK END

                    INGRID
          Your dad would be proud of you for following him in your foot's steps.

Donna extends his hand while flinching as Ingrid extends her hand.

                    DONNA
     Hi.

                    INGRID
          You must be Grant's mother.

                    DONNA
              (changing voice pitch)
          Yes. I'm such a proud mother.

                    INGRID
          Is Don still missing?

DONNA
(changing voice pitch)
I miss him.

INGRID
You must believe he'll return.

GRANT
(whispering)
You must be a blond.

INGRID
Yes! The ancient one was right. The Blind Archer can see!

GRANT
Oh brother.

Grant's cellphone rings.

DONNA'S PAGER BUZZES: 911

20

SHE'S ALREADY DEAD, DON'T PANIC?

INT. FUNERAL HOME - DAY

Donna and Grant stand over Rubee's lifeless body in a casket.

                    GRANT
          Whatever happened to mom?

                    DONNA
          It's simple. She left.

Donna starts to tell the story of his mother.

DONNA'S FLASHBACK

EXT. UPPER STATE NEW YORK HIGHWAY - MORNING

SUPER: JUNE 6 - 6:56 AM - TWENTY-NINE YEARS AGO

Don Davis, before he got the title, "Bullseye," is running down the highway mountain topless, long hair flowing while showing off his muscular physic and bright smile.

The sun glimmers off Don's pecks.

> DONNA (V.O.)
> I was minding my own business while I was running when I saw a car flipping over the turnpike. So I immediately ran over.

Don Davis lotions up his pecks while running in slow motion on purpose.

> DONNA (V.O.)
> Then I saw her.

EVE, twenties hot strapping body, toned in every inch of her muscle, stumbles out of her flipped car with nothing but a few cuts and scraps.

> DONNA (V.O.)
> She stood there for what felt like eternality. Our eyes locked.

Eve rips off her top, showing off her sexy physic, walks right up to Don Davis.

Eve, showing off her SHIBA INU tramp stamp tattoo and falls onto Don's arms.

> EVE
> Lets make a baby.

Eve looking at Don's eyes passionately.

> DONNA (V.O.)
> I was headed to my first competition that morning, but then your mother, at the time, distracted me. I found myself grabbing her and riding off into the sunset on a unicorn.

Both Don and Eve are topless and riding on a unicorn into the clouds.

      GRANT (O.S.)
 What happened?

      DONNA (V.O.)
 Then you were born, and she was gone.

Don is holding BABY GRANT riding alone on a unicorn headed into a hurricane.

Sunlight shines on both of them as they disappear into the hurricane.

END DONNA'S FLASHBACK

21

COFFEE GINGER PIZZA
Chapter

INT. FUNERAL HOME - DAY

Rubee's eyes open up

      RUBEE
 Lier!

Rubee jumps out of the casket and does a 180 superhero flip landing.

      RUBEE
 You are just a scared little boy hiding under all that woman?

Rubee is attacking Donna with multiple kicks and punches, which is why Donna is having a hard time dodging Rubee's attacks.

      DONNA
 I'm sorry, Mamma.

      RUBEE
 No, you're not you pathetic choice of a man. You couldn't stand up to the crypto gang, yet you can be an ultimate fighter. Once again, mama's boy is in trouble.

      DONNA
 I'm sorry, Mamma.

				RUBEE
	Sorry? Have you noticed how Grant now talks to his dog like a human. You officially made him crazy like you.

Donna is having a panic attack.

Rubee never jumped out of the casket and Donna is imagining all this.

				LAPORSHA
	Shit!... He's having a panic attack.

				RUBEE (O.S.)
	Good. Have a panic attack and grow a pair.

				GRANT
	Dad.

LaPorsha pulls out some edible cookies.

				LAPORSHA
	Give him some edibles to help calm him down.

				GRANT
	You got edible cookies?

				LAPORSHA
	What you need?

LaPorsha pulls out edibles, weed, cocaine, meth, cigarettes and a bottle of Whiskey.

				LAPORSHA (CONTINUOUS)
	I got you covered.

INT. LAWYER OFFICE OF GINGER - MORNING

Grant, LaPorsha, and Donna are all sitting in Ginger's office. GINGER, 48 big husky dark black man who is always eating.

COFFEE, during the daytime works as an office assistant and at night goes by the moniker "COFFEE" at Jiggly Jiggly walks in with six pizza boxes.

                    COFFEE
        Your 10 am pizza has arrived.

Coffee places the pizza boxes and 2-liter coke in front of Ginger.

Ginger opens up the first pizza box and starts to eat.

                    GINGER
       Would you two like a slice?

Grant, LaPorsha, and Donna start eating a slice of pizza.

Ginger closes the folder while eating.

                    GINGER
      Rubee Davis left you nothing.

                    DONNA
Nothing?

Ginger opens up second pizza box.

                    GINGER
     She did leave a video instructions.

Ginger takes the remote and clicks the television on.

ON TELEVISION

                    RUBEE
Dan, son. I have taken care of your outstanding debt with the crypto mafia. I leave my business to my great-grandson Bingbong. I was in the red and unsure if he wanted it since he is working on becoming a chef and as for Grant. I'm leaving you my motor-chair. If you keep bumping into things, you're going to need it sooner than later. I guess if you are watching this, I made my last bet and lost.

Ginger pausing the video while drinking out of the 2 liters.

                    DONNA
I thought you said she left nothing.

                    GINGER
To you.

                    LAPORSHA
What a waste of time.

                    GINGER
She did place her final bet.

                    GRANT
What does that mean?

                    GINGER
She placed 10k on 4-1 odds that the 76ers will win tonight's game, sweeping the title from the Clippers.

                    DONNA
Who gets the money if she wins.

GINGER
Not you.

GRANT
Who?

GINGER
You

GRANT
Me?

GINGER
Yes, you. Minus my fees, of course.

DONNA
Explain this again?

GRANT
If the 76ers sweep the Clippers on game 4 of the NBA Finals, grandma will win 40k.

GINGER
76ers are favored to win. Just come by tomorrow to pick up the check.

LAPORSHA
What happens if you lose?

GINGER
Don't bother showing up if they lose. Our time is over. My assistant will see you out the door.

GRANT
What about the last part of the video.

GINGER
Oh, I totally forgot.

Ginger unpauses the video.

ON TELEVISION

                    RUBEE
If I win, I was going to pay for that eye surgery you keep talking about. Just remember that I'm proud of you for your accomplishments. You don't need eyes to see. Those 76ers better win. They're favored.

22

INT. UNKNOWN VEGAS LOCATION - DAY

SUPER: VEGAS

The all-white oval room has a Matrix vibe with over 600 monitors playing every kind of sports imaginable on every screen all around the room.

At the center of the room is VEGAS, a figure cloaked by a white robe hidden by the only darkness in the room, the center of the room.

                        COMPUTER A.I. (V.O.)
        Vegas. There's been a high level of bet placed on
        the 76ers game tonight. A high probability of Loss
        will incur.

Vegas grabs the only thing on the table. A RED CELLPHONE with a screensaver reading, "House always wins."

The Red Cellphone automatically starts dialing.

INT. WELLS FARGO CENTER - NIGHT

A packed arena watching The Los Angeles Clippers take on the Philadelphia 76ers.

Sixers Philadelphia, MATT CORD announces the game.

                        MATT CORD
        This has been a hella of a battle tonight. The
        Clippers are fighting with their last breathe to
        keep alive tonight. If Ben Simmons and Joel
        Embiid can keep their composure tonight. They
        would sweep the Clippers. It's been a long
        journey. The last time 76ers won a championship
        since 83'

INT. AMEER'S TAVERN - NIGHT

There is a hip tavern where everyone's attention is towards the big screen playing the Philadelphia 76ers vs. The Clippers NBA FINALS.

Grant, LaPorsha, and Cindy sit in a booth together while watching the game.

                  GRANT
Thank you for taking me here.

                  CINDY
So if the 76ers win tonight. You win 40k?

                  GRANT
I can't believe it either.

INT. WELLS FARGO CENTER - NIGHT

                  MATT CORD (O.S.)
You better start believing, folks. Tyrese Maxey's three-point shot just put the 76ers over the Clippers. 112 to 106 with 51 seconds remaining on what is to be called the greatest game thus far.

INT. AMEER'S TAVERN - CONTINUOUS

                  LAPORSHA
You have one of the weirdest lucks I've ever seen.

Grant, super-excited, starts to cheer.

                  GRANT
Want to go with me to Vietnam?

                  CINDY
I love to travel.

                  LAPORSHA
I'm staying. I hear they eat dogs.

GRANT
(towards LaPorsha)
They don't eat dogs.

CINDY
Is that where you are going to have your surgery?

GRANT
I want you to be the first thing I see.

LAPORSHA
Look at you all romantic and shit.

INT. WELLS FARGO CENTER - CONTINUOUS

The lead REFEREE ERIC, 40 white, cellphone buzzes in his pocket.

Referee Paul taps his earpiece.

VEGAS
It's time.

INT. AMEER'S TAVERN - CONTINUOUS

CINDY
Awe. You're so sweet.

The crowd at Ameer's is getting louder by the second.

CINDY
Lets stop by Germany on the way back and do some traveling together.

INT. WELLS FARGO CENTER - CONTINUOUS

JOEL EMBIID, power forward for the 76ers, misses an easy shot, and SETH CURRY retrieves the ball.

The crowd boos.

> MATT CORD (O.S.)
> The crowd is defiantly letting Seth Curry know their distaste for him leaving to play for the Los Angeles Clippers this season.

Seth Curry runs with the ball and immediately shoots a 3-point shot.

> MATT CORD (O.S.)
> Seth Curry for three.

Referee Eric blows the whistle.

> MATT CORD
> Foul on the call. Seth is headed to the line and has not once missed a free throw in this NBA Finals.

Seth Curry makes all three free throws.

INT. AMEER'S TAVERN - CONTINUOUS

The crowd is yelling at the Referee.

> CINDY
> Come on!

> GRANT
> What's the score.

                        CINDY
109. 112. 76ers leading by three with ten seconds remaining.

                        LAPORSHA
I have been wrong before.

                        CINDY
Ten seconds.

                        GRANT
                (whispering to himself)
Come on, come on. Come on.

Crowd chanting 76ers to win!

INT. WELLS FARGO CENTER - CONTINUOUS

Clippers forward PAUL GEORGE makes an easy lay up, scoring two points.

                        MATT CORD (O.S.)
Ten seconds on the clock. It's now 111. 112. One-point game, and Tyrese Maxey has the ball.

Referee Eric blows the whistle.

                        MATT CORD (O.S.)
The whistle has been blown, and it looks like it's a personal foul on Joel Embiid. Lets look at the replay.

INT. AMEER'S TAVERN - CONTINUOUS

The crowd quiet, looking at the replay.

ON TELEVISION

Embiid light taps Seth Curry's forearm.

The crowd starts to scream at the Referee.

INT. WELLS FARGO CENTER - CONTINUOUS

Joel Embiid, pissed, walks up to Referee Eric.

> JOEL EMBIID
> Yo man, I thought we were boys.

> MATT CORD (O.S.)
> Embiid is voicing his opinion to Referee Eric tonight.

Referee Pauls takes a small step forward to Joel Embiid.

> REFEREE PAUL
> Step back, Joel.

> JOEL EMBIID
> (pointing at Eric)
> You need to get your eyes checked, Eric.

Joel Embiid's fingertip slightly touches Referee Eric.

The 2ND REFEREE blows a whistle.

> MATT CORD (O.S.)
> It looks like it's a personal on Embiid. This is his 5th, and he's done.

> JOEL EMBIID
> This is bullshit!

Joel Embiid takes off his jersey and walks towards the exit.

All the fans near the exit stage start to chant Embiid's name.

                    76ERS FANS
We love you Embiid!

The crowd screams at the referees as Seth Curry takes the ball.

                    MATT CORD (O.S.)
With Embiid fouled out. The Clippers have the ball with six seconds left.

Seth does a layup and makes the basket.

                    MATT CORD (O.S.)
Foul on the play. It looks like it's another foul on Seth Curry, this time by point guard Tyrese Maxey. Two points count as Seth Curry goes to the free-throw line. He's one player that shouldn't be fouled. He hasn't missed one all night long. And he's back on the line.

Seth Curry makes the free throw.

                    MATT CORD (O.S.)
It's a tie with the layup. 112 to 112 with 3 seconds remaining. Seth Curry hasn't missed, and the 76ers fans in Wells Fargo Center are making noises hoping for his first miss.

Seth Curry makes the free throw.

                    MATT CORD (O.S.)
And it's good. 113-112, Clippers. Three seconds remain. Simmons has the ball.

BEN SIMMONS, Point Guard for the 76ers, receives the ball and immediately throws it from half-court.

GAME OVER BUZZ

The crowd is upset.

      MATT CORD
Airball. Game over. Upset in Philadelphia tonight.

      MAN IN CROWD (O.S.)
The ref is fucking blind!

INT. AMEER'S TAVERN - CONTINUOUS

      TAVERN PATRON (O.S.)
Fucking Vegas!

      CINDY
Once again, the referee called the game.

      GRANT
Once again. No longer going to keep my hopes up.

      CINDY
You'll win tomorrow.

      GRANT
I got to now.

LaPorsha is playing pool.

      LAPORSHA
Good luck, kid.

      GRANT
Are you coming tomorrow?

CINDY
I wouldn't miss it for the world. Want to come over so we can go together.

GRANT
I can't. Have to drop off my grandmother's ashes in Canada with my father.

Cindy runs her finger from the tip of Grant's head to his crotch.

CINDY
Then I shaw see you tomorrow afternoon.
(beat)
Mr. Archery Champion.

Cindy squeezes her hand.

Grant flinches because Cindy squeezes his crotch a bit too hard as she kisses his neck.

LaPorsha continues to play pool by herself while smoking.

LAPORSHA FLASHBACK

LaPorsha has multiple flashbacks of getting kicked out of multiple homes.

BACK TO SCENE:

LaPorsha does a line of cocaine on the pool table.

23

OH CANADA!
Chapter

INT. ABOB'S CAR - MOVING - MORNING

Grant is in the driver's seat while LaPorsha is steering. Donna is holding his mother's urn.

                    DONNA
      We're almost there.
           (beat)
      I told you it would be quick.

                    GRANT
      If you so strapped for cash. How did you come up with five thousand so quickly?

FLASHBACK

Donna smashes a man's head to the ground multiple times during one of his underground fights.

                    DONNA
           (yelling)
      Who's the bitch now?

Donna is smashing the same man's head against another man's head.

                  DONNA
            (screaming)
    Is he your bitch now?

                          END OF
                        FLASHBACK

                  DONNA
            (calmly)
    Teaching archery.

                  GRANT
    You suck at it.

                  LAPORSHA
    He defiantly does.

EXT. CANADA BORDER - MORNING

Grant parks the car in front of the Canada's gate.

Everyone is waiting outside.

                  GRANT
    Now what?

                  LAPORSHA
    Someone's coming.

                  DONNA
    They'll be here soon, son. It's just the last stop for grandma.

Canada's Prime Minister JUSTIN TRUDEAU walks up to Donna.

Donna gives the urn to Justin Trudeau.

> **LAPORSHA**
> What is the prime minister doing picking up your grandmother?

> **GRANT**
> Justin Trudeau is picking up the ashes?

> **DONNA**
> Yes. You're starting to use your gift.

> **GRANT**
> It's not a gift. I keep telling you, LaPorsha is talking to me.

> **DONNA**
> All I hear is bark bark bark bark.

> **LAPORSHA**
> (Channels Wanda Sykes)
> That's because your a dumbass you motherfucker. You confused white boy!

> **DONNA**
> Let go. Your destiny awaits.

> **LAPORSHA**
> Destiny? I feel like I'm in a movie and I just witnessed a walk-on role.

EXT. ROADSIDE - MOMENTS LATER

Thirty miles in the middle of nowhere.

                    GRANT
          Did we run out of gas?

                    LAPORSHA
          What am I now? Fuck, I gotta do it all now?

                    DONNA
          I think these are hybrid.

                    LAPORSHA
          Not helpful.

                    GRANT
          Let's chill.

                    LAPORSHA
          Shit, you try chilling the fuck out with fur on.

                    GRANT
          I'm going to miss the competition.

                    LAPORSHA
          The one.

                    GRANT
          Oh, shut the fuck up.

                    DONNA
          Talking to your dog was cute initially, but now I feel you might have some mental issues?

                    GRANT

Mental? Thanks, mom, I mean, dad. Or it. Doesn't fucking matter. I can't see none of you two anyways!

Grant starts to walk away.

GRANT
So fuck you!

LAPORSHA
You're going to get run over!

GRANT
Awesome!

DONNA
Come back.

LAPORSHA
You know what... I'm done.

LaPorsha walks the opposite way.

DONNA
You two are acting like children.

LAPORSHA
Fuck you.

GRANT
Fuck you.

DONNA
Are we done?

LAPORSHA
No.

GRANT
No.

Grant hasn't moved more than 6 feet and is standing in the middle of the road.

LaPorsha just moved 6 inches and starts to smoke a bong hit while pouring herself another shot of Whiskey.

GRANT
I'm going to miss my one shot too...

LAPORSHA
Might as well just leave me.

GRANT
Where did that come from.

LAPORSHA
I'm use to it now.

GRANT
I'm not going to leave you.

DONNA
The dog isn't going to leave you.

LAPORSHA
You mean that?

GRANT
I'm talking to you aren't I.

DONNA
You can also talk to me Son.

LAPORSHA
You got a strange family kid.

GRANT
You're part of it.

LaPorsha and Grant start to walk back together as they are about to hug one another.

Out of nowhere, SNIPERS hit Grant, LaPorsha, and Donna with sleep darts.

THE CRYPTO GANG Chapter

INT. CRYPTO-GANG DUNGEON - DAY

Both Grant and LaPorsha wake up tied to a chair.

Donna still knocked out, is tied to a standing roulette rack in front of Grant and LaPorsha.

> GRANT
> Are you ok, LaPorsha?

> LAPORSHA
> Sorry, it looks like be late to your competition.

> GRANT
> What else is new. I'm just happy that you're ok.

> LAPORSHA
> I'll help you find another way.

> GRANT
> Where's my dad?

> LAPORSHA
> Well, She-man is currently tied to the wheel of fortune.

Grant tries to break free from the rope.

GRANT
Where are we?

DOGE, male and SHIBA INU, female -both have faces of a Shiba Inu dog breed attached to human body dressed in business suits.

DOGE
You're in crypto!

SHIBA INU
Crypto bitches.

LAPORSHA
You got to be kidding me, where'd these two white boys come from, Gawddamit!… is this in the fucking script anymore?!

SHIBA INU
We don't kid, we de-fi.

GRANT
You can hear her?

DOGE
We hear all.

SHIBA INU
We know all.

GRANT
What do you want?

DOGE
We hear that you have been in contact with Don "Bullseye" Davis.

GRANT
I haven't seen my father in years.

SHIBA INU
Don't you lie to me, boy!

DOGE
We have ways of finding out.

LAPORSHA
Hear all and know all? Nigga please, what you bitches want?

GRANT
His debt has been paid.

DOGE
Yes but, he still owes.

GRANT
What does he owe?

SHIBA INU
Transaction fees

LAPORSHA
You know what, Fuck you and your dip.

Doge shoves a Kabosu in LaPorsha's mouth and muzzles her.

Donna wakes up and is not surprised.

DONNA
The Crypto Gang.

DOGE
Where's your husband?

>   DONNA
>   (Change voice)
>   I don't know

>   DOGE
>   Of course, you don't.

>   GRANT
>   And I'm the blind one.

LaPorsha desperately tries to talk.

>   SHIBA INU
>   The Blind Archer. I thought we would make this
>   interesting, especially for you.

Doge points at the release lever for Donna's standing roulette rack.

>   DOGE
>   If you can hit the release lever without the help of
>   your dog. Then you are free to go.

>   GRANT
>   If I miss?

>   SHIBA INU
>   You die.

Shiba Inu points at Donna

>   SHIBA INU
>   She dies.

Doge pushes the lever making Donna's roulette rack spin round and round.

>   DOGE

> You all die!

There's a knock on the door.

ELON MUSK just lets himself in and walks up to Doge and Shiba Inu to deliver them ice cream.

> ELON MUSK
> (hugging Doge and Shiba Inu)
> What's going on, guys.

Doge licking his double chocolate chip ice cream.

> DOGE
> Here's the deal.

> GRANT
> How much does my dad owe?

> DOGE
> One thousand dollars.

LaPorsha rips off her muzzle.

> LAPORSHA
> One thousand dollars?

Shiba Inu eating ice cream.

> SHIBA INU
> One thousand dollars.

Grant is eating ice cream.

> GRANT
> One?

Elon Musk is eating ice cream.

                ELON MUSK
       Just one thousand guys?

Grant licking his ice cream cone.

                GRANT
       You drugged us, tortured us.

Grant licks his ice cream cone.

                GRANT
       And you were going to kill us.

Grant licks his ice cream cone.

                GRANT
       All for one fucking grand?

Grant frustratingly pulls out his bow and arrow and immediately shoots the arrow towards Doge, SHIBA INU, and Elon Musk.

Doge blocks the arrow, which ricocheted off of Doge's paw bracelet, and hits the release lever for Donna's standing roulette rack.

Donna falls to the ground, trying not to throw up.

LaPorsha is now eating ice cream.

                DOGE
       I see the tails of the Blind Archer are true.

                SHIBA INU
       However, this does not settle your father's debt.
       Blind Archer!

						DOGE
If we find him.

						SHIBA INU
We will kill him.

						GRANT
Over 1 thousand dollars? Unfucking believable.

LaPorsha eating ice cream.

						LAPORSHA
This POTUS special edition flavor is delicious. I almost forgot where I'm at.

SNIPERS out of nowhere shoot knockout darts at LaPorsha, Grant, and Donna.

One of the knockout darts hits Elon Musk in the neck.

Elon Musk, still in between Doge and Shiba Inu, pulls out the small dart.

						ELON MUSK
					(towards Doge and Shiba Inu)
Was all this really necessary?

Elon Musk looks at the camera and takes his last lick of ice cream while rolling is eyes.

25

00 ABOB Chapter

EXT. ROADSIDE - DAY

LaPorsha, Grant, and Donna wake up next to Abob's Tesla.

Donna is still a bit dizzy.

                    DONNA
        Give me one second, son.

                    GRANT
        Take all the time you need. We'll be here awhile.
        I'm going to take a piss.

                    LAPORSHA
        Good idea. Me too.

Grant pulls down his pants and starts to take a piss.

Grant's Cellphone Rings.

Grant picks it up.

The Wind blows the piss back into Grant's face.

INT. AIRPORT HANGER - DAY

Abob is having a shootout with 6 HENCHMEN.

                ABOB
I wanted to call and wish you luck today at your finals.

Abob returns fire and ducks behind airport crates.

                GRANT
Not going to be able to make it.

                ABOB
What happened.

                GRANT
Stuck out in the middle of nowhere. One hundred twenty miles, and I'll never make it in a car.

Abob returns gunfire, killing two Henchmen.

                ABOB
It sounds like you need to be air-born.

                GRANT
Why do I hear gunfire.

Abob jumps over one of the airport crates while breaking one of the Henchmen's neck in the process.

                ABOB
I'm at work.

                GRANT
Ugh.

                ABOB

>   Don't ugh me. Negativity is a killer.

Abob shoots Two Henchmen in their face, killing them.

>   GRANT
>   I'm not pessimistic. I'm a realist. The only way I
>   would make it on time is if I could fly.

Abob returns gunfire towards the last Henchmen.

Abob looks behind him and sees - The Sikorsky X2, a high-speed compound helicopter.

>   ABOB
>   How about a jet helicopter.

INT. HELICOPTER - DAY

Abob jumps into the Helicopter and returns fire.

>   ABOB
>   The Sikorsky X2 is an experimental high-speed
>   compound helicopter with coaxial rotors
>   developed by Sikorsky Aircraft. Top speed: 299
>   mph Range: 807.8 mi Cruise Speed: 286 mph
>   Engine type: LHTEC T800. This girl will get you
>   anywhere you want lickily split.

>   GRANT
>   What is it that you do you again?

Abob jumps into the helicopter pilot seat, turns on the engine, and takes off.

The last Henchman, YUG DAB, runs and jumps onto the rails of the helicopter, hanging onto the helicopter's rails.

The Helicopter flies out of view.

ABOB FLASHBACK

A YOUNG ABOB sees a job flyer posted on the job bulletin board at his residence hall at college.

CU - JOB FLIER

                    ABOB (O.S.)
Remember that job interview I had in college.

Want to be a DOUBLE O. If you have the determination and enjoy traveling perks, email M at careers@00.com

We do have a high rate of turnovers because we are looking for the best of the best. Join our team.

                    GRANT
The night manager position at McDonalds?

                    ABOB
No the other one. Anyways it doesn't matter right now. I'll tell you all about it when we aren't so rushed.

                    GRANT
Do you think we have time?

                    ABOB
Think. No. Remember to think position and always
            (beat)
Look up.

Abob's helicopter appears above Grant, LaPorsha, and Donna.

Abob's helicopter is lowering down slowly.

                    LAPORSHA
     Is that your friend coming in
           (beat)
     Helicopter?

                    GRANT
     Yes. I might make it.

                    LAPORSHA
     I thought I seen it all.

EXT. ROADSIDE - DAY

The Helicopter is hovering next to Donna, Grant, and LaPorsha. Evil Henchman Yug Dab is still hanging onto the helicopter rails.

                    ABOB
     Jump in. Hurry up. Lets go!

The helicopter flies towards the mountains while Evil Henchman Yug Dab hangs on for dear life.

26

BINGBONG BOOMER
Chapter

MONTAGE OF BINGBONG - DAY

A) Bingbong opens the refrigerator door and pulls out the frozen 10k he has been saving behind Grant's frozen eyes that are still in the pickle jar.

B) Bingbong pays a man for his used Food Truck.

C) Bingbong gets his picture taken.

D) Food truck gets a new paint job with BingBong's face vinyl onto the side of the Food Truck.

E) Bingbong tweets his new business. BingBong's Cuisine.

EXT. VERMONT STATE FAIR - DAY

The 71st Annual World Archery competition in Rutland, Vermont at the state fairground with hundreds of spectators in the stands cheering as MACK CHAZY, a very hairy Jamaican with dreads to his waist, grabs the mic.

                  MACK CHAZY
Grant Davis has six minutes to report to the judges, or he will be disqualified. Please report to the Archery grounds.
            (beat)
While we wait, enjoy some good quality food at one of our many food truck vendors available. My favorite this year is Bingbong cuisines.

EXT. BINGBONG'S MOBILE CUISINE FOOD TRUCK - DAY

Bingbong's face is on his food truck with the wording, "Bingbong's Cuisine."

BOOMER DANG, an 8-year-old white boy, shows his order code on his phone.

> BOOMER
> Pick up for two orders of Bing Pho. Two orders of Bing Banh xeo and two orders of Bing Bun bo Hue.

Bingbong sticks his head out the food truck window.

> BINGBONG
> Delivery?

> BOOMER
> Pick up.

> BINGBONG
> That's a lot of Vietnamese food for a white boy family.

> BOOMER
> Well, apparently, I'm mixed, and it's for my family.

> BINGBONG
> I'm mixed too, but I don't buy it.

> BOOMER
> Why not?

> BINGBONG
> I don't look anything like my father and never met my mother.

BOOMER

I don't look anything like my parents either but, I love them even though they gave me a messed-up name.

BINGBONG

What's your name?

BOOMER

I always got teased for my name.

BINGBONG

Me too until I read online how to empower yourself with the name that was given to you at birth.

BOOMER

I'm Boomer.

Bingbong hands Boomer his orders.

BINGBONG

I'm Bingbong. Thank you for your patron, look forward to seeing you again.

192

27

Chapter

MACK CHAZY

EXT. JUMBOTRON - CONTINUOUS

A video plays on the Jumbotron.

Mack Chazy appears on the Jumbotron.

                    MACK CHAZY
     America has fallen

Huge text appears, "AMERICA HAS FALLEN."

The American Eagle has an arrow impaled in its body.

                 MACK CHAZY (CONTINOUS)
   But, we Americans don't give up.

Mack gives mouth-to-mouth resuscitation to The Eagle.

                 MACK CHAZY (CONTINOUS)
    We Americans fight!

Mack, dressed in a doctor's lab coat, is doing emergency surgery on the American Eagle.

>   MACK CHAZY (CONTINOUS)
>   We fight to our last breathe

Mack Chazy is punching The American Eagle, trying to get him to wake up.

>   MACK CHAZY (CONTINOUS)
>   We Americans are resilient.

The American Eagle wakes up and is now in a full-body cast.

>   MACK CHAZY (CONTINOUS)
>   And when life kicks us down. We stand up

Series of Video Shots

A) Mack Chazy removes the body cast.

B) The American Eagle hangs out on Mack's shoulders.

C) The American Eagle gives Mack butterfly kisses.

>   MACK CHAZY (CONTINOUS)
>   We stand up and say not today. Not today

Series of Photo Shots

A) Mack and The Eagle watching the TV show LOST

B) Mack and The Eagle sharing a blunt

C) Mack and The Eagle sleeping together

>   MACK CHAZY (CONTINOUS)
>   America is the land of opportunity where we can
>   be free

The American Eagle lands on Mack's arm.

Fireworks appear behind Mack Chazy, posing with The Eagle.

28

EXT. ROADSIDE - DAY

LaPorsha, Grant, and Donna wake up next to Abob's Tesla.

Donna is still a bit dizzy.

DONNA
Give me one second, son.

GRANT
Take all the time you need. We'll be here awhile. I'm going to take a piss.

LAPORSHA
Good idea. Me too.

Grant pulls down his pants and starts to take a piss.

Grant's Cellphone Rings.

Grant picks it up.

The Wind blows the piss back into Grant's face!

INT. AIRPORT HANGER - DAY

Abob is having a shootout with 6 HENCHMEN.

ABOB
I wanted to call and wish you luck today at your finals.

Abob returns fire and ducks behind airport crates.

GRANT
Not going to be able to make it.

ABOB
What happened.

GRANT
Stuck out in the middle of nowhere. One hundred twenty miles, and I'll never make it in a car.

Abob returns gunfire, killing two Henchmen.

ABOB
It sounds like you need to be air-born.

GRANT
Why do I hear gunfire.

Abob jumps over one of the airport crates while breaking one of the Henchmen's neck in the process.

                    ABOB
          I'm at work.

                    GRANT
          Ugh.

                    ABOB
          Don't ugh me. Negativity is a killer.

Abob shoots Two Henchmen in their face, killing them.

                    GRANT
          I'm not pessimistic. I'm a realist. The only way I
          would make it on time is if I could fly.

Abob returns gunfire towards the last Henchmen.

Abob looks behind him and sees - The Sikorsky X2, a high-speed compound helicopter.

                    ABOB
          How about a jet helicopter.

INT. HELICOPTER - DAY

Abob jumps into the Helicopter and returns fire.

                    ABOB
          The Sikorsky X2 is an experimental high-speed
          compound helicopter with coaxial rotors
          developed by Sikorsky Aircraft. Top speed: 299
          mph Range: 807.8 mi Cruise Speed: 286 mph
          Engine type: LHTEC T800. This girl will get you
          anywhere you want lickily split.

GRANT
What is it that you do you again?

Abob jumps into the helicopter pilot seat, turns on the engine, and takes off.

The last Henchman, YUG DAB, runs and jumps onto the rails of the helicopter, hanging onto the helicopter's rails.

The Helicopter flies out of view.

ABOB FLASHBACK

A YOUNG ABOB sees a job flyer posted on the job bulletin board at his residence hall at college.

CU - JOB FLIER

ABOB (O.S.)
Remember that job interview I had in college.

Want to be a DOUBLE O. If you have the determination and enjoy traveling perks, email M at careers@00.com

We do have a high rate of turnovers because we are looking for the best of the best. Join our team.

GRANT
The night manager position at McDonalds?

ABOB
No the other one. Anyways it doesn't matter right now. I'll tell you all about it when we aren't so rushed.

GRANT
Do you think we have time?

ABOB
Think. No. Remember to think position and always
(beat)
Look up.

Abob's helicopter appears above Grant, LaPorsha, and Donna.

Abob's helicopter is lowering down slowly.

LAPORSHA
Is that your friend coming in a
(beat)
Helicopter!

GRANT
Yes. I might make it.

LAPORSHA
I thought I seen it all, but this could take the cake and my eyes!

EXT. ROADSIDE - DAY

The Helicopter is hovering next to Donna, Grant, and LaPorsha. Evil Henchman Yug Dab is still hanging onto the helicopter rails.

ABOB
Jump in. Hurry up. Lets go!

The helicopter flies towards the mountains while Evil Henchman Yug Dab hangs on for dear life.

INT/EXT. HELICOPTER - DAY

ABOB Flying the helicopter while Grant, LaPorsha, and Donna holding onto their seat belts.

Evil Henchman Yug Dab crawls back into the helicopter and pulls out a samurai sword.

                    YUG DAB
          You think you can get away from me so quickly,
          Abob.

Yug Dab pulls out a semi and starts shooting towards Abob

Donna, using her left breast, knocks the semi out of Yug's hand and uses her right breast to uppercut Yug.

Abob and Donna start to fight against Yug Dag as the helicopter begins to fall towards the ground.

                    ABOB
          Take the controls, Grant.

Grant is having a hard time unbuckling.

                    ABOB
          Grant!

LaPorsha, face-plant while shaking her head. She pulls out her flask and takes a big shot. She runs towards the helicopter controls and is a bit puzzled.

Yug steps on Grant's face while Abob stands on Grant's face.

Donna throws a parachute at Abob, who uses it to block Yug's sword stab.

Donna, Abob, and Yug are stepping all over Grant as they fight. Grant continues to unbuckle, yet the many kicks to his body snap the buckle back to lock position.

PILOT SEAT

                        LAPORSHA POV
A Mountain and helicopter's controller are flicking colors as it falls.

                        BACK TO SCENE:

LaPorsha takes out a huge blunt and, with much calmness, takes a big hit.

                        LAPORSHA
                 (pulls back on controls)
Fuck it!

                        ABOB POV
Abob sees a West Highland White Terrier dog pulling back the controllers while smoking a blunt.

                        BACK TO SCENE:

INT. HELICOPTER - CONTINUOUS

                        ABOB
Well, that's something you don't see every day.

Abob gets punched in the face by Yug.

>	DONNA
> We're not going to make it.

Donna gets kicked in the grown.

>	LAPORSHA
> (calmly smoking)
> Shut the hell up, She-man.

Donna laughs as Yug continues to kick her groin.

Yug slaps Donna and side-kicks Abob.

Yug throws multiple ninja stars towards the remaining parachute.

>	YUG DAB
> Till we meet again.
>	(beat)
> Abob.

Yug dab jumps out of the helicopter and pulls out a gun from his ankle. Shoots the helicopter's fuel line.

>	LAPORSHA
> (smoking calmly)
> We're running out of fuel.

LaPorsha successfully brings the helicopter over the mountain.

>	LAPORSHA
> We're going to have to land pretty soon.

>	GRANT
> I've missed the finals.

ABOB
(looks at his watch)
You still have time.

GRANT
How much time?

ABOB
Remember the saying focus on yourself.

Abob starts to put a parachute on Grant.

GRANT
What's happening?

ABOB
Think positivity... no matter what!

Abob walks Grant to the edge.

GRANT
No... I can't do it.

ABOB
You have no choice. You only have 30 seconds left, or you lose.

GRANT
I can't

ABOB
Focus on the things you can control and not the things you can't.

GRANT
Like what!

                    ABOB
                (pushes Grant)
         Like opening up the parachute

                    GRANT
                  (falling)
              I'm fucking blind!

EXT. MID-AIR - CONTINUOUS

Grant's parachute's strap rips.

INT. HELICOPTER - CONTINUOUS

Donna is holding the only parachute without ninja stars on it.

                    DONNA
            You gave him the wrong one.

                   LAPORSHA
         Son of a bitch. I'm starting to like that kid.

DONNA'S POV

Donna sees a West Highland White Terrier dog smoking weed and holding the helicopter's controls.

The West Highland White Terrier lets go of the controllers, jumps out of the seat, runs towards Donna's hand, and steals the parachute.

The dog jumps out of the plane.

                              BACK TO SCENE:

                  DONNA (CONTINOUS)

Well, that's something you don't see every day.

Donna and Abob stay puzzled, looking at LaPorsha holding the parachute while skydiving towards Grant.

The helicopter is slowly descending.

EXT. MID-AIR - CONTINUOUS

GRANT
Oh my god, I'm going to fucking die.

LAPORSHA
Keep it together.

LaPorsha straps the parachute on Grant and skydives into his arms.

Grant grabs onto LaPorsha and yanks the cord.

GRANT
Teamwork.

EXT. VERMONT STATE FARM - CONTINUOUS

MACK CHAZY
Ten seconds.

Grant releases the parachute.

Helicopter explodes in the backdrop while Grant does a front flip, superhero-style landing while throwing LaPorsha behind him into his quiver.

GRANT
(a-just his eye bandana)
I'm here.

CROWD GOES WILD

209

EXT. BINGBONG'S MOBILE CUISINE FOOD TRUCK - DAY

                      BOOMER

That's so cool!

                      BINGBONG

That's my dad

Bingbong takes a photo and immediately post it to

BINGBONG'S TWITTER

Bingbong posted a photo of Grant's superhero landing position with the tweet, #TheBlindArcher That's my father."

Mack Chazy walks up to Grant as he stands up.

                MACK CHAZY
       Do you know what they are calling you now?

Grant nods no.

                MACK CHAZY
       The Blind Archer!

The American Eagle swoops down and steals the sunglasses off of Vick Thompson, who is wearing a New York Yankee Hat while taking a selfie with Suzy Grant.

The American Eagle circles the sky above the State Fair.

                MACK CHAZY
       Archers to your positions.

All the FINAL ARCHERS line up to their starting position while a GLARE from THE SUN shines a-pond them all.

                MACK CHAZY
       We will find out who's the top archer with a grand prize of one hundred thousand dollars in SHIBA INU sponsored by Coinbase.

LaPorsha puts on sunglasses.

                LAPORSHA
       It's bright as fuck. I can barely see. I swear the white devil motherfucker, be the death of me.

GRANT
If you can't see, how am I going to do this?

LaPorsha pours herself another Whiskey shot.

LAPORSHA
Once again. Take a chill pill. You got this.

Every single Archer is missing the target because of the glare of the sun's rays bouncing off of The American Eagle's sunglasses who is flying around the and competition.

MACK CHAZY
This is the first time I have ever witnessed so many archers missing the target. It's defiantly a bright day in Vermont.

LAPORSHA
I'm going to need a bigger bottle.

LaPorsha pulls out a Whiskey bottle and starts to drink it.

GRANT
Stop drinking. I need your help.

LAPORSHA
I can't help it. I drink when I'm and nervous.

LaPorsha falls out of Grant's quiver with the bottle.

LAPORSHA
I'm ok.

GRANT
LaPorsha. Help.

The glare of the sun shines bright in LaPorsha's face.

LAPORSHA
It's too fucking bright. I can't see shit.

GRANT
So, I'm doing this blind?

LAPORSHA
Everyone else is as well.

All the Archers keep missing their target.

MACK CHAZY
No points on board for no one. Every archer has shot zero for five except Grant Davis. I wonder what he is waiting for. If The Blind Archer doesn't shoot in the next few minutes, he will be disqualified.

All the Archers shoot their arrows, and all the archers miss the target completely.

MACK CHAZY
No points on the board. It's a tie score. Zero for six, and The Blind Archer is Zero for Zero.

Grant pulls out a vape and takes a deep inhale.

Grant pulls out an arrow from his quiver and starts to hear different voices in his head.

ABOB (V.O.)
You can do this.

SUZY (V.O.)
You're nothing but a loser.

RUBEE (V.O.)
Yes, you can.

CINDY (V.O.)
Archery is in your blood.

                  SUZY (V.O.)
You're lousy in bed

                  DONNA (V.O.)
You are the one.

                  LAPORSHA
You got this, kid.

Grant pulls back on the arrow.

30

BROKEN BOW

FLASHBACK

EXT. VERMONT MOUNTAIN - MORNING

Donna walks up to Grant and places the Arrow he caught in Grant's hand.

                DONNA
    Now turn around, take a deep breath

Grant aligns the arrow turns around.

                DONNA
  Listen to the air, hear the leaves, feel the wind.
  Use your other senses besides your sight.

Grant listens to the wind and aims the arrow at LaPorsha.

LAPORSHA
Aim it at your 9 o'clock.

Grant adjusts his aim and releases the arrow.

Grant lands his first bullseye.

LAPORSHA
Holy shit, you did it!

GRANT
I did?

DONNA
You always could.

GRANT
How?

LAPORSHA
Yeah, how the fuck did he do that?

DONNA
You're the one, son.

LAPORSHA
Ask your she-man father how the fuck did the arrow just changed directions on a dime.

GRANT
How did the arrow land on the target if I completely missed?

DONNA
You're the chosen Archer. The one archer that the wind bends and serves your will. You'll never miss. The chosen archer will be able to communicate with the wind.

GRANT

The wind?

DONNA

Stop focusing on sight and focus on nature around you. Did you feel that aurora of cold wind tickling every part of your body when you were holding the arrow?

GRANT

Yes.

DONNA

Next time focus harder by letting go and feeling the wind talking to you. The aurora feelings will let you know when it's ready to let go.

END OF FLASHBACK

GRANT PULLING BACK THE ARROW

LAPORSHA (O.S.)

Just fucking shoot it already.

GRANT'S BOW BREAKS.

The Crowd gasp

31

The Crowd gasp

                    MACK CHAZY (O.S.)
The Blind Archer's bow broke.

                    GRANT
   Fuck.

                    LAPORSHA
What do we do now?

Ingrid, about to shoot her sixth arrow, stops and starts walking towards Grant.

MACK CHAZY (O.S.)
It's looking like Ingrid, the Swedish sensation is
withdrawing from the competition.
          (beat)
And she's walking towards The Blind Archer?

The Crowd, scared, starts looking towards the sky in panic mode.

                    LAPORSHA
Why are boobies walking towards us?

INGRID FLASHBACK

EXT. VERMONT STATE FAIR - DAY

SUPER: 5 YEARS AGO - 66TH ANNUAL WORLD ARCHERY COMPETITION

The 66th Annual World Archery competition in Rutland, Vermont at the state fairground with hundreds of spectators in the stands cheering.

INGRID 25, cellphone rings.

CU - INGRID'S CELLPHONE

VEGAS CALLING

Ingrid ignores and continues to shoot her arrow.

INT. UNKNOWN VEGAS LOCATION - DAY

                      VEGAS
Vegas doesn't leave messages.

Vegas pushes a button on his Red Cellphone.

EXT. VERMONT STATE FARM - CONTINUOUS

Ingrid's cellphone rings.

CU - INGRID CELLPHONE

VEGAS IS CALLING

Ingrid answers the phone hesitantly.

                      INGRID
    I understand.

CU - INGRID CELLPHONE

NEW MESSAGE - UNKNOWN

A photo of Ingrid's father and mother being held up by gunpoint.

MESSAGE: YOU KNOW WHAT TO DO

                                BACK TO SCENE:

EXT. VERMONT STATE FARM - CONTINUOUS

                    INGRID
              (whispering to herself)
    I'm sorry, Don.

Ingrid shoots her last Arrow at the target while walking up to Don "Bullseye" Davis.

                    INGRID
    Bullseye!

Ingrid lifts her top, exposing her huge 36DDD breast.

Ingrid's left breast punches Don's face. Ingrid's right breast uppercuts Don's face.

Don releases the arrow.

END OF FLASHBACK

                                        BACK TO SCENE

32

THE BLIND ARCHER

INT. VERMONT STATE FARM - DAY

Ingrid takes her bow and offers it to Grant.

                        LAPORSHA
        She looks like she's giving you her bow.

                        GRANT
Who?

                        INGRID
A friend.

                        MACK CHAZY (O.S.)
    It looks like Ingrid is no longer in the competition
    and The Blind Archer is back.

Grant feels out the new bow.

                        MACK CHAZY (O.S.)
    Now isn't this exciting, folks!

The crowd goes wild.

Grant starts to feel the aurora around him as all the hairs on his arms start to flicker.

                    THE WIND
So you're the one?

Grant gets startled.

                    THE WIND
The one. The one who decided to piss on me.

                    GRANT
Who's there?

                    LAPORSHA (O.S.)
It's me... Hurry up and shoot it.

                    THE WIND
Don't let go of the arrow so soon. Look. I'll be quick about it because the last one, they put her in the loony bin because she kept talking to me. So do yourself a big favor and shut the fuck up and just listen, goddamit.

                    GRANT
Ok

                    LAPORSHA (V.O.)
Ok!

                    THE WIND
You're the only archer in the world that can save this planet from blab blab blab from end of times blab blab blab and be the savor of this world yadda yadda yad. I have been doing this for thousands of years, and that part of the prophecy is ludicrous.

GRANT
So you're saying I will never miss?

THE WIND
It only works when you're blind. I don't make these rules, so don't get all torn about it. Just don't talk to me in public because people will think your crazy, just like those idiots who talk to their dogs thinking that they're having a meaningful conversation.

LAPORSHA (O.S.)
You can still miss. Just move the arrow slightly to the right.

THE WIND
Trust you can do it, and I'll make it happen. Just don't ever piss on me again.

GRANT
(whispers to himself)
Bullseye.

Grant releases the arrow.

The arrow looks like it's going to miss way off.

LaPorsha sighs as she takes another long shot from her Whiskey Bottle.

A HUGE GUST OF WIND pushes the arrow downwards.

Grant's arrow hits the bullseye.

MACK CHAZY
Bullseye. We have a bullseye. We finally have an archer that hit the target.

              LAPORSHA
         Hurry up and keep shooting!

All the archers get blinded by the glare of the sun bouncing off of The American Eagle's sunglasses once again.

              MACK CHAZY
         All archers miss again. It's zero for seven. Blind Archer one.

Grant pulls out another arrow.

              THE WIND
         Just shoot the dam thing.

              LAPORSHA
Shoot.

              GRANT
         (whispers to himself)
         Bullseye.

Grant pulls back and releases.

The WIND pushes the arrow.

              MACK CHAZY
         Bullseye. The blind archer is 2-0

              LAPORSHA
         Keep shooting.

Grant pulls out another arrow shoots.

              MACK CHAZY
         Bullseyes again from the Blind Archer. 3-0

All the Archers are on their ninth arrow.

The Glare of the sun blinds all the archers again.

All the Archers miss their targets again.

                MACK CHAZY
   All archers are missing their targets. It's 0-9. Blind
   Archer 3-0.

Grant pulls out SIX ARROWS and aligns them on his bow.

                GRANT
            (whispers to himself)
   Bullseye in each target.

LaPorsha drops her Whiskey bottle.

                LAPORSHA
   I stand corrected.

Grant shoots all SIX ARROWS at once.

                GRANT
            (whispers)
   Bullseye.

                MACK CHAZY
   Now, this is something you don't see every day.

Grant hits the bullseye with all six arrows. Each of the six arrows hit bullseye on six different targets.

                MACK CHAZY
   Bullseye. Bullseye. Bullseye. Bullseye. Bullseye.
   Bullseye. Six bullseyes. Holy snickers Six. That's
   out of this world!, folks.

Grant grabs the baseball that has been in his pocket for years and throws it at the sky.

Grant immediately pulls out an arrow and shoots the baseball in mid-air.

The Crowd goes wild.

                    LAPORSHA
          Showing off much.

BULLSEYE'S BACK!

The American Eagle lands back on Mack Chazy's shoulders and adjusts his sunglasses.

>					MACK CHAZY
>		The winner of the 100k SHIBA INU 71Th Annual
>		Archery Competition sponsored by Coinbase is
>		the one, and only, Grant "The Blind Archer" Davis!

The Crowd goes wild.

>					GRANT
>				(talking to the wind)
>		Thank you.

>					THE WIND
>		What did I say? Are you also a mute.

The Wind exhales on Grant causing his hair to be tattered by the wind.

>					THE WIND
>		You're welcome, kid. Just remember that I'm
>		always around you. I can do more than just blow
>		your arrows to their targets, if you know what I
>		mean.

LaPorsha jumps onto Grant's arms.

                      LAPORSHA
    We won!

LaPorsha and Grant successfully high-fived each other again.

                      GRANT
    I'm happy that you chose me.

                      LAPORSHA
    Best friend ever.

LaPorsha and Grant hug.

                      LAPORSHA
    I know you can't see them, but turn around so that at least you can acknowledge their support.

Grant turns around

                      GRANT
    Who?

LAPORSHA'S POV

Donna is jumping up and down, Bingbong taking photos, Cindy blowing kisses, and Abob giving a thumbs up while grabbing his cellphone out of his pocket.

Grant thanks and acknowledges LaPorsha's help.

ABOB has disappeared again!

                                      BACK TO SCENE

WINNER'S CIRCLE

Doge and Shiba Inu walk onto the winner's circle holding a sign that reads: Congratulations Blind Archer.

JUMBOTRON

We see a sideshow presentation of 100k in SHIBA INU.

We see a live crypto blockchain 100k being transfer into Grant's Coinbase Account.

The animated advertisement for Coinbase text reads: Grant Davis can now spend or invest his 100k in Shiba Inu winnings in seconds thanks to blockchain technology and brought to you by Coinbase for Shiba Inu.

Mack Chazy places a 1st place Medal over Grant's head.

Mack Chazy pumps up the crowd.

The Crowd goes wild.

Donna jumps up and down excited for his son and rips off his wig.

                       DON "BULLSEYE" DAVIS
Bullseye's back!

Doge and Shiba Inu look at the camera.

                                     FADE TO BLACK.

                                       DISSOLVE TO:

34

I SEE YOU

Chapter

EXT. SKY - DAY

747 Airplane is descending fast. One of the engines catches on fire.

EXT. NETHERLANDS - DAY

SUPER: SOMEWHERE IN THE NETHERLANDS

747 airplane crash lands.

All the passengers and crew members walk out of the plane through the smoke and fire.

EXT. NETHERLANDS - MOMENTS LATER

EVE, Grant's birth mother, walks out of the 747-plane crash unhurt with only a few cuts, bruises, and ripped clothing. We can see Eve's SHIBA INU tramp stamp tattoo thru her ripped clothing.

EXT. NETHERLANDS ROADSIDE - DAY

The 747 plane is a few hundred feet away.

A Blue Volvo Station Wagon appears out of now where.

INT/EXT. BLUE VOLVO STATION WAGON - DAY

ADAM GARDENA, 51 accountant looking gentleman who has seen better days, rolls down the window.

ADAM GARDENA
Are you ok, miss?

EVE
(interrupting)
Lets make a baby.

EXT. NETHERLANDS ROADSIDE - CONTINUOUS

Eve enters Adam's Volvo station wagon, and Adam drives off into the distance.

INT. HOSPITAL CLINIC - MORNING

SUPER: HANOI, VIETNAM

Doctor See Lee looks into the camera, pulls out a flashlight, and shines the bright light at the camera.

We can hear multiple Nurses and Doctors speaking in Vietnamese in the background voicing their concerns at this significant eye surgery that is about to happen.

DOCTOR SEE LEE

Doctor See Lee see problem. You no have eyes. We fix. We clean. First, We put old eye in, connect wires, pray and rest. No problem, I can do for you.

Doctor See Lee, picking his nose, turns off the flashlight.

Doctor See Lee puts on his glasses and starts to laugh like a mad man.

DOCTOR SEE LEE

I see you.

The Doctor covers the camera with a blood-stained towel.

FADE TO BLACK.

Doctor See Lee continues to laugh uncontrollably.

DOCTOR SEE LEE (V.O.)

I see you.

FADE OUT

HOW THE BLIND ARCHER CAME TO BE

Have you ever had an idea and thought about how stupid it was, then the next day you keep thinking about that stupid idea, and you share the stupid idea with your friend who questions the concept with multiple stupid questions? And the next day, you come up with the answer to those multiple stupid questions. What turned out to be a one-stupid line joke grew to a sentence. As days go by, the stupid idea starts to form a life of its own, birth by stupidity. The life force of this stupid idea keeps getting stronger and more muscular, and all those so-called innovative, cool concept ideas that I wanted to write were just silenced by this one stupid idea. The more stupid questions I had, the more I got interested in this stupid idea because this character just grew. My friend Ryan told his wife, Que, about the idea, and she got curious and had questions to which we had answers, and they were equally stupid.

After two weeks, I just decided to write an outline but thought to myself that I just didn't want to waste my time with this stupid idea and didn't want to have my time wasted. Then that night, while listening to music, I thought to myself and asked myself one question. How would I have sold this idea to myself when it kept me laughing and interested for two weeks. So, I thought I do something entirely different for myself. Write to sell, finish for self.

Write to sell, finish for self. What I mean by this is. I told myself that I would write the synopsis first as if my focus was to sell it. And once that part is done. I will finish it for self means that I'm going to enjoy writing this screenplay with one focus. To have a sample of my writing and a spec script added to my resume would hopefully land me a screenwriting job to write for a movie studio or sell this script. It would be nice if both. I have more than one script but, I guess the more, the merrier. So, I started to write a logline and synopsis to see if I could sell this particular concept to myself. Without an outline, I wrote the synopsis and logline. It took me longer than expected.

I wanted to see a poster for some odd reason once I finished and knew it would be a great idea to add it to the synopsis. A mock-up of what the movie poster would look like for The Blind Archer helped me write and kept me on track. I'm not the greatest artist but, I can sketch semi-good. Sadly, I didn't keep practicing when I was younger, but I thought that a mock-up poster would benefit my idea of selling it, no matter how it came out. So, I did a mock-up as if it were instruction for another artist.

The synopsis helped me write the outline faster than I expected. I left empty slots here and there for plot development. I was about to write when I thought I should come up with all the characters' names in the outline to avoid wasting valued time. I called my writing friend Jeff and asked for name opinions. He asked questions, and with a bit of tug and pull, I decided to tell him the basic idea, and he immediately laughed, which felt like I was onto something. I have to give Jeff Bonilla credit for naming one of the characters. Bingbong. Other than the basic idea premise, I have not shared the idea with anyone else because I wanted to focus on one thing now: finish it.

Do I have any actors in mind when coming up with this idea? Yes. I have two actors in mind. Ingrid, the Swedish sensation's character, I envision Dolly Parton playing the role. I know what you're thinking. Ingrid is portrayed as a 25- and 30-year-old but, I have complete confidence that Dolly can portray it correctly, plus I had Dolly in mind. Plus, it is great to get her on the soundtrack, hint hint. As for the other character, I did write LaPorsha for a specific actress. When LaPorsha's character popped into my vortex, Wanda Sykes immediately came to my mind. I know she can add her style and make LaPorsha's character her own in her performance. Plus, she's black; wait, is that too insensitive to say? Hey Wanda, if you're reading this, big fan! Hugs.

I started to write seamlessly and even found myself writing scenes out of order. I was getting to page 50 when I was more focused on finishing but stopped a few days till I had friends in the much older crowd stop by and visit. All I had in my mind was LaPorsha and The Blind Archer. They asked what I was writing, and I decided to pitch the idea. I told them the basics and explained the concept has dark humor, but they laughed at every scene I was describing. Hearing the laughter gave me the motivation to push forward and finish it.

This idea has evolved yet again. I decided to use this screenplay as a spec script. I also decided that I would try and sell this script or any one of my others. I need a literary agent or manager which I also plan to use this script to obtain representation. I also am going to upload the script into iBook and Amazon. Why not, I asked myself. It is exciting to have this script in my hands like a book. My first-time art mock-up of the poster has been growing on me every time I look at it. The poster will be my book cover for the script where anyone can read it. I trip out on the artwork because, at first, I wasn't a fan, yet the poster art style grew on me. I stopped writing for a day to design the back cover, keeping to the style of the front.

I'm at page 89, and I'm getting a sense of anticipation on almost finishing. I have only two scenes left to write, and I will be done. I'm shooting for 100 pages but, I would be happy with 91 pages. I had to stop and write this because I sometimes wonder what my thought process was when I came up with this stupid idea—laughing aloud by myself. After all, there are plots, subplots, reasons, and themes. If after reading "The Blind Archer," you were curious about the inception of the story and wanted to know much more, keep reading; on September 15, 2021, and for two weeks, the idea grew with Ryan Whiteoak helping shape the idea as we both continued to laugh about the scenarios. I started to write the screenplay on October 1, 2021.

Today is Monday, October 18, 2021, and I'm just two scenes away from finishing, The Blind Archer. I have been writing every day for the past 18 days. Some days I write for 4 hours a day, others may be longer. Each day was different in hours but, I accomplished something every day. On days that I just needed a small break, I found myself designing the posters for the second and third movie of The Blind Archer. I found myself writing a quick paragraph of each sequel. The next thing I knew, I was writing down scenes that would work for the sequel, and one character that was supposed to be in the first just didn't have enough space for this one character to breathe. This character is even on the poster, but my name covers his identity, so the design cover works in a funny way. Once I do an edit and read through, I will defiantly upload this story online. I just find it hilarious that this once stupid idea is now a fully fledge screenplay story.

If you are curious about how long the whole process took me. It took me 36 days from idea to concept to finished script with a poster design. I will most likely have the book uploaded and start to get representation in about 7-10 days from today.

It's Wednesday, October 20, 2021, at 12:34 am, exactly as I type this.

I have been living in Vermont for the past month and a half, and I must say that writing this screenplay, "The Blind Archer," will be one of many memories I will always carry with me from Vermont.

It took me just two extra days. I decided to take a break for the day, and I felt confident that I started to work on the last two scenes the next day. I even added one additional scene. The last and final scene I wrote for The Blind Archer is a musical number for LaPorsha. First time writing lyrics but, it was fun visualizing Wanda Sykes dancing and singing. I don't want to ruin this scene but, it's a scene that defiantly has to be in the movie because I'm confident you won't forget this specific scene.

Thank you for joining me on this adventure.

Enjoy,

Ray Mond

10/20/2021

The Blind Archer

ABOUT THE AUTHOR

RAY MOND

After my successful years of writing and teaching, I became a motivational speaker for fortune 100 companies worldwide. I teach how I get so much done in a day. I call it Ray of Focus. Example: Getting, The Blind Archer screenplay, synopsis, book, and designed all in 30 days. I accomplished this task, using "Ray of Focus"

What else can I say about myself that the world hasn't already known about me for years. World-renowned writer, actor and comedian. I travel the world in search of the best chocolate chip cookies. I like to give back during the winter by teaching one English class at the University of Yalle at Gotham City, focusing on sarcasm.

Currently, I'm very proud to say that I'm the private trainer of Kim Jong-un, Supreme Leader of North Korea. In 2020, I had to change my focus because my good friend called me and desperately needed a trainer, and I promised him I will get him the best trainer in the world, Six minutes later, I went to LAX to book a flight to North Korea to focus on getting Kim back into a lean, mean fighting machine. It's been a long 2020, but I am happy to announcing that he is now lean, mean and ready to conquer 2021 and beyond.

As I wait at Pyongyang International Airport to head back to America, I will start focusing. Focus on 2022 is to get The Blind Archer into production while doing my motivational speaking tour. If things go well, My rap album will be released on iTunes Christmas 2022.

I love tips, batman, pho, tips, pop culture, music and did I mention tips? :)

yes, this is my real crypto paystring. Able to get the username "thebatman" has to be one of the proudest moments of my life. Bucketlist, one checked off.

In today's Info Overload Wars, I thank you for spending a little bit of time with me.

thebatman$paystring.crypto.com

Ray Mond

255

Made in the USA
Middletown, DE
20 April 2023

29208486R00151